## His eyes roamed over her body insolently

Sensuously James touched the fabric covering her breasts. "Real silk," he drawled admiringly. "Women wear expensive nightwear either to entice a lover or because it is a gift from some doting male. Which is true in your case, Tara?"

"Neither," she said furiously. "I don't—" Just in time Tara caught herself almost admitting she had never had a lover—or ever wanted one—apart from him. "Look, James," she went on huskily, "this has gone far enough. I'd like you to leave or—"

"Or what?" he goaded her. "You'll scream? I think not."

Tara stared up at him wildly. James was like some dark catalyst, disturbing the even pace of her life, forcing to the surface all the deep swirling currents she had fought to subdue.

PENNY JORDAN
is also the author of these

# *Harlequin Presents*

Many of these books are available at your local bookseller.

For a free catalog listing all titles currently available,
send your name and address to:

HARLEQUIN READER SERVICE
1440 South Priest Drive, Tempe, AZ 85281
Canadian address: Stratford, Ontario N5A 6W2

# PENNY JORDAN

## phantom marriage

*Harlequin Books*

TORONTO • NEW YORK • LOS ANGELES • LONDON
AMSTERDAM • PARIS • SYDNEY • HAMBURG
STOCKHOLM • ATHENS • TOKYO • MILAN

Harlequin Presents first edition May 1983
ISBN 0-373-10591-6

Original hardcover edition published in 1983
by Mills & Boon Limited

Printed in U.S.A.

# CHAPTER ONE

IF she didn't hurry she was going to be late picking the twins up again, Tara acknowledged, glancing in resignation at the heavy-duty watch which looked so incongruous against the fragility of her wrist.

Today Chas has been more difficult than ever. Twice he had had the model in tears, and only her own deft soothing had enabled them to carry on.

It was not merely luck and knowing the right people that had taken Chas to the top as a fashion photographer, and even when she was appalled at the brutal, uncaring way he treated his models, Tara still found it possible to admire his skill, and the driving desire for perfection his unyeilding determination evidenced.

Today he had been particularly savage, and not just with the model, and Tara knew the reason why. Ever since she had started working for him as his personal assistant he had made hio dooire for her very evident. In a way she knew she ought to be flattered that he wanted her when so many beautiful girls were only too ready to share his bed, but then Chas was cynical and hardbitten enough to know that his models were only too happy to sleep with him if it meant it would further their career, whereas she ... She stifled an impatient sigh as he gave terse instructions to her regarding the development of some of the shots he had taken. Photography had always been one of her interests, and when she had been left alone after the twins were born she had turned to it as a means of earning a living. Eventually she hoped to have a studio of her own, and this she had made plain to Chas when she first went to work with him. As far as work went she couldn't fault him. He was marvellously patient in showing her all the tricks of the trade and helping her with her own photography; unstinting with both genuine praise and genuine criticism, and was now allowing her to take on some of their more routine work entirely unsupervised. An ad they had done for stockings several weeks ago had brought a positive paean of praise from the client, and Chas had given her full credit for her work. No, it was not where work was concerned that Chas was becoming impossible. In a way it was almost ludicrous that he should find her desirable; at twenty-four and the mother of six-year-old twins she had long ago ceased thinking of herself as the object of any man's desire.

'And don't forget, we've got that weekend assignment coming up,' were Chas's final words as she hurried to where her car was parked.

It was an assignment Tara was privately dreading. They had received a commission to take some fashion shots at Leeds Castle which would take up an entire weekend. Tara had protested that she couldn't possibly leave the twins, but Chas had overruled her, saying that his housekeeper would be delighted to look after them for her. The real reason she didn't want to go was that she sensed that Chas would use the weekend to force her into an affair with him—an affair she didn't want, but offending him might ultimately mean losing her job, which she enjoyed very much and which was extremely well paid.

Sighing, she eased herself into her ancient Mini, adjusting the driving mirror as she did so, pausing as she caught sight of her own reflection. Twenty-four; she grimaced wryly. She didn't look it, which was ridiculous when she remembered that at eighteen she had looked older. Eighteen . . . She grimaced, tossing the thick length of her brown-blonde hair off her shoulders. Normally she wore it in one single plait for work but this morning they had overslept and there hadn't been time. Her face free of make-up belied her years, freckles standing out plainly across the bridge of her nose. Her hair had a natural tendency to curl, tiny tendrils feathering across her forehead. Her eyes were an unusual mixture of hazel-green; hazel one moment, jade green the next, in accordance with her mood. As a child she had been volatile, given to impulsive gestures, but age and experience had cured her of that.

She switched on her engine, groaning mildly as she glanced again at her watch. Her skin was faintly tanned still from a trip she had made to Greece with Chas earlier in the year. Her mother had looked after the twins for her, but grudgingly. She had never really got over the fact that they had been born illegitimate. Tara grimaced as she pulled out into the main stream of traffic. It had not been purely for the twins' sake that she had invented a 'deceased husband' for herself when she moved to London shortly after their birth. As she had quickly discovered in the months following their arrival, while some areas of 'sophisticated' society now quite happily condoned the birth of children outside marriage, in male eyes there was still

an element of the 'fallen woman' attached to girls who
admitted to fatherless children, and Tara had grown
sick of the men who had offered friendship and
affection merely because they assumed her unmarried
mother status meant they would quickly gain access to
her bed. They had soon learned their mistake, just as
she had quickly learned from hers. She had left the
small town where she had gone to stay with her aunt
and uncle to await the birth of the twins, and started
anew in the safe anonymity of London where no one
cared enough to question her youthfully widowed
status.

It had been a lucky move. She had managed to get
the twins enrolled at an excellent nursery, while she
herself had gone to college to complete the education
so rudely shattered by the discovery of her pregnancy.
It had been impossible for her to go to university,
but she had gained a sound grounding in secretarial
work, which had meant that at least she had been able
to earn enough to keep a roof over their heads. An
unexpected Premium Bond win had provided the
money for the deposit on the small terraced house she
had bought in what had been a very unfashionable
part of London, but which was now fast moving up-
market as more and more young couples made it their
home, and there had been sufficient money left for her
to afford the fees at the small private kindergarten the
twins were attending. This last expense was a bone of
contention between Tara and her mother. Her mother
had moved to the same town as Tara's aunt and uncle
after the twins' birth, complaining bitterly that she
could no longer stand the shame of living in the same
place that had witnessed her daughter's disgrace.

Tara's father had been killed in a road accident when Tara herself was five and she could barely remember him, so her mother and her aunt and uncle had been the only family she had known. All three of them now felt uncomfortable with her, she acknowledged, and so her visits to them were infrequent. Her mother considered private education to be morally wrong, but Tara had pointed out to her as gently as she could that she wanted the best for the twins.

When she had first discovered that she was pregnant her mother had wanted her to have her child adopted, but Tara had remained adamant that she wouldn't. There had been no possibility of marriage to their father, of course. Her eyes darkened, the fingers gripping the steering wheel suddenly white. Oh how that still hurt after all these years when surely she ought to have put it long behind her, but James's total rejection of her still had the power to wound. It wasn't even as though he had the excuse of being a young innocent as she had been herself. An unwillingness to face up to his responsibilities was something she could have understood and accepted in a boy of eighteen, but in a man of twenty-seven . . . As always when she thought of James bitterness welled up inside her. The first time they met she hadn't realised what was to come. He had simply been the father of a younger school friend.

Memories suddenly threatened to come crowding back, and with the skill of long experience, she dammed them up, concentrating on her driving and the evening ahead.

It wasn't far from the studio to the kindergarten, which was one of the reasons she had chosen it.

To her relief there were still other cars parked outside when she arrived; mothers waiting to collect their offspring, and she smiled in wry amusement, acknowledging the incongruity of her shabby Mini amongst so many luxuriously expensive boxes on wheels.

An elegant blonde woman smiled at her as she eased herself from the Mini. Tara smiled back vaguely, eyes searching the playground for the twins' familiar dark heads, and a small pent-up sigh escaped the full warmth of her lips when she spotted them playing on the slide.

Outwardly neither twin bore the slightest resemblance to her; both had inherited their father's darkly attractive looks, softened by baby chubbiness, and an undeniably coquettish femininity in the case of Mandy.

Tara grimaced a little as she thought of her pretty, wilful little daughter. Already the little girl seemed to exhibit a perverse delight in thwarting her mother, and Tara recognised unwillingly in the little girl's behaviour a need for the firm and loving hand of a father. Mandy was all female and had been from the moment of her birth, just as Simon was a sturdy miniature replica of his father. Like Mandy he too suffered the lack of a father, although in Simon it showed more in the pensive seriousness of his eyes and his tendency to cling a little too much to the protection afforded by Tara.

Simon as always saw her first and came running over to her, flinging his arms round her jean-clad knees, while Mandy followed in his wake, dark curls flying.

'You're late,' Simon accused when she had kissed them both.

Tara sighed. 'I know, darling.'

'Is Uncle Chas coming round tonight?' Mandy demanded. Chas occasionally popped round in the evening to discuss work, and Mandy tended to disapprove of his visits.

As Tara was explaining to them that it was unlikely, the blonde woman who had smiled so tentatively at her before suddenly approached with a toddler, her smile deepening to recognition as she came closer.

'Tara!' she exclaimed in pleased accents. 'I *thought* it was you.'

She mustn't have looked at her properly the first time, Tara decided, suddenly feeling ill, otherwise she would have recognised her instantly, despite the sophistication that seven years and the apparent addition of a wealthy husband had given.

'Susan.'

Did her voice sound as weak as she felt?

'What a fantastic coincidence,' the other girl chattered on blithely, obviously unaware that Tara wasn't sharing her pleasure. 'It must be at least seven years since I last saw you. You never even told me that you were leaving Hillingdon,' she added reproachfully. 'Are these your children?'

'Yes.'

Tara was desperate to escape, but it was impossible while Susan admired the twins, and picked up her own toddler, who, she informed Tara, was just three and was called Piers.

'After his grandfather,' she added, pulling a slight face. 'Do you know, I just can't get over meeting you like this. Of course the chauffeur normally collects Piers from school. What are you doing with yourself ...' Her eyes slid to the betrayingly ancient state of Tara's Mini in comparison to her own elegant BMW. 'You married, of course ... Your husband ...'

'John died before the twins were born,' Tara lied huskily, bending down to check the fastening on Simon's shoes, glad of the excuse to hide her expression from the girl who had once been one of her closest friends. Why did this have to happen? Why did she have to run into Susan of all people like this?

Susan was instantly sympathetic.

'Oh, you poor thing!' she exclaimed, glancing significantly at the twins as she added, 'No problems there, I hope? I can still remember what the lack of a father did to me, although it wasn't the same thing. Mother divorced my real father when I was four. I don't suppose I ever mentioned that to you before—I hated people knowing. She's remarried again, you know,' she added conversationally, patently unaware of the sudden tensing of Tara's body. 'The older she gets the younger her husbands get. She's living in the States now. I think of all the fathers she provided me with James was my favourite. In the old days I never used to admit he wasn't my father. He was wonderful fun, do you remember ...?'

Did she? Tara forced a smile from a face that felt as though it would crack apart and expose her anguish to the world and managed to croak, 'Yes ...'

'Look, we must get together,' Susan announced

enthusiastically. 'We've so much to catch up on. We've just bought a house in the country—for Piers mainly. At the moment we can only use it at weekends, although his father is hoping to transfer his business down there eventually. We're going down this weekend, why not come with us? The twins would love it, I'm sure.'

'I . . .'

'Don't refuse,' Susan begged. 'Think about it. Here's my phone number.' She scribbled it down on a piece of paper and handed it to Tara. 'I couldn't believe it when you left Hillingdon like that, although I suppose at fourteen I was really too young for you to take me into your confidence. But you'd been so marvellous to me at school; like the sister I'd never had. Do you remember? You seemed to know instinctively how I felt about the problems I was having with Mother. I suppose that was something we shared, although for different reasons. Do you, like me, want to give your two all the love and affection we never had?' She broke off as she realised that her car was blocking an exit, hurrying Piers towards it, calling over her shoulder to Tara, 'Now don't forget—you're spending next weekend with us!'

All the way back to the house Tara felt completely numb. Susan of all people! She had spoken the truth when she said that they had had much in common. Susan had been one of the juniors at school when Tara was a prefect. She was always in trouble; stubborn, rebellious, undisciplined, but beneath her outward brashness, her seeming precocity, Tara had recognised the same inner despair and vulnerability she felt herself. It hadn't been an easy task breaking down the barriers of years to discover the real Susan. The supposed sexual exploits which had so shocked one of her form teachers had, as Tara had suspected, been no more than fabrication; but there had been a great danger that Susan would fall into the trap of promiscuity in the intensity of her search for someone to give her the love and security she craved. To nullify the effect of a mother who was too distant and wrapped up in her own needs and desires to see what was happening to her child.

They had grown very close; as close as sisters, as Susan had claimed. When she had discovered that Susan was often left completely alone in the huge barn of a house which was only one of Mrs Harvey's homes, Tara had taken to spending the occasional weekend with her. She herself had been studying for A-levels then, and following her example Susan had started to take a much keener interest in her own work. 'A miniature do-gooder,' had been one of the less cruel tags Susan's mother had applied to her, because despite her lack of interest in her child, Mrs Harvey had been bitterly resentful of Susan's friendship with her.

In those days she had known very little about Susan's background. Her mother and father were seldom at home; in fact the first time she had met Susan's father she hadn't realised who he was. It had been during one of the weekends she had spent at Susan's home. She had woken in the night and wanted a drink. Downstairs in the kitchen she had been on the point of opening the fridge when she realised she wasn't alone. Fear had been quickly followed by curiosity when she had realised that the tired, gaunt-looking man slumped over the kitchen table was the fabled father Susan adored, and an oddly maternal wave had swamped her when he raised his head and looked at her with exhausted eyes.

She had cooked him a meal; she recalled it vividly. He had eaten without appetite, and it was only years later, suffering from jet lag herself, that she had realised just how unwelcome her ministrations and cooking had probably been, but he had been too kind to let her see it. James had a weakness for children and lame dogs, but the trouble had been that she hadn't been a child, although neither of them had realised it until too late.

'Mummy, I'm hungry!'

Mandy's imperative cry broke through her thoughts. Tiredly she switched off the car and helped them out. The casserole she had prepared that morning before leaving for work smelled appetising as they walked into the kitchen. Sending both twins upstairs to change their clothes and wash, Tara set about preparing their meal. Although five o'clock was rather early for her to eat, she preferred to share her meals with the twins rather than eat alone; vivid memories of lonely meals eaten in solitude at the kitchen table while her mother looked on a strong deterrent against subjecting her own children to the same thing.

Mealtimes were normally the highlight of her day. Over their food the twins normally regaled her with the happenings of their day, and she made a point of listening seriously. Simon normally spoke with wide-eyed solemnity but Mandy, almost too quick for her own good, could easily spot when an adult was simply indulging her.

They came downstairs together dressed in identical dungarees.

'Simon couldn't fasten his sneakers,' Mandy told her, 'so I had to do it for him.'

Suppressing a sigh, Tara inspected their newly washed hands. It was quite normal for Mandy to be more advanced than her brother at this stage, she knew, but she was concerned that Mandy's possessively maternal attitude to her brother, although delightful, might prevent Simon from learning to stand on his own two feet.

Both children ate hungrily. Tara was an excellent cook and mainly through firm insistence in their early years, neither twin was faddy about food. Her budget might not stretch to luxury items, Tara reflected, but at least the twins had a well balanced and healthy diet; and as far as she was concerned they were far better off without too many sweets and chocolates.

Mandy promised to have her own slender build, but already Simon was heavier, and she suspected he would grow up to resemble his father.

After dinner she always set aside an hour to play with the twins and read to them. Mandy with quicksilver impatience grew bored with reading, but Simon was always anxious for more. Almost identical in looks, by nature they were vastly different, Tara reflected.

Her mother had started a campaign obviously intended to steer her towards marriage; its benefits to the twins always stressed whenever she went home, but so far Tara had resisted. For one thing, marriage would mean telling someone about the twins' paternity, which she had no desire to do; for another it meant exposing herself once more to their rejection.

Other girls, she knew, suffered the same experience she had done without the same results, but then she had always been acutely sensitive; too sensitive, she acknowledged, recognising that some of her fear for Simon sprang from the fact that she feared he had inherited this vulnerability from her.

It seemed almost incredible now that her body had ever experienced the aching pleasure which was now only a dim memory, but which had once driven her to forget all her principles and scruples to the extent that nothing mattered save for James's possession of her, even though she had known quite well that at the time his actions were blurred and his mind dazed by a lethal combination of exhaustion and jet lag.

Not a pretty memory, and one which had served to help her keep a cool control over her emotions ever since. He loved her, James had said, but his later actions had not borne out those words. What he had felt for her had simply been a momentary desire, and she, fathoms deep in love with him, had encouraged and incited him into making love to her. The twins were the result of that careless lovemaking, and on them Tara had poured out all the love she had been forced to bottle up inside her.

Casual affairs were just not her thing, and while there had been plenty of men who had made it plain that they desired her, Tara had always held them at a distance. So far Chas had been the most determined, but Tara had held her ground, and it gave her no pleasure to know that Chas's sudden spurts of temper against the models were fuelled by sexual frustration caused by her refusal to sleep with him.

So far she had managed to walk the dangerously fine line of keeping their personal relationship completely separate from work. As a photographer Chas was a professional down to his fingertips, but Tara worried that one day he would break what was obviously a self-imposed rule, and remind her that he had it in his power to make her unemployed. So far he had not used that weapon, and she honoured him for it. However, there was this weekend job coming up involving taking some fashion shots at Leeds Castle. She had racked her brains for a legitimate excuse for not going, but so far none had been forthcoming. The twins could go with them, Chas had said easily when she commented that she could not simply abandon them for an entire weekend.

It came to her that Susan's invitation would provide a cast-iron excuse for refusing to go; it would also prevent Chas from guessing her fear that if she simply refused the assignment he would press his suit even harder, forcing the confrontation she had so far managed to avoid.

# CHAPTER TWO

THE morning didn't get off to a good start. For one thing, Tara's alarm failed to go off on time, and she was eventually woken up by Mandy tugging impatiently at the bedclothes.

Tara normally got up an hour before the twins, using the time to wash her hair and do her make-up. Although far from vain she considered presenting the right image an important part of her job, although sometimes it was hard to strike the narrow dividing line between appearing too glamorous or too staid. Normally she settled for simply keeping her hair clean and glossy, using the minimum amount of make-up and dressing in clothes that didn't impede her work and yet still looked smart.

This morning there was no time to wash her hair, and she plaited it quickly while she supervised the twins' breakfasts.

Simon for some reason had decided that he loathed boiled egg and was morosely engaged in pushing his sulkily round his plate.

'Simon, eat up!' Exasperation sharpened her voice and she sighed when the little boy's face crumpled.

'I'm sorry, darling.' A swift hug and a kiss banished the threatening tears, although Simon was obviously not going to let her off easily.

'My tummy hurts,' he complained. 'Mummy, I

don't want to go to school. Why can't I stay at home with you?'

'Because I have to go out to work,' Tara told him firmly, surreptitiously checking his pulse and temperature. Both seemed normal. Simon's pain was more imaginary than real, she suspected, and sympathised with him, remembering how often she had suffered similar afflictions.

'Are we going to stay with that lady for the weekend?' Mandy demanded as Tara bustled them outside to the Mini. 'Where does she live?'

'I don't know,' Tara was forced to admit. 'In the country somewhere.'

'The country?' Simon perked up immediately. 'On a farm?' he breathed hopefully.

Although it was ridiculously early to be worrying about careers for the twins, Simon's very evident love of the countryside and its inhabitants led Tara to believe that he would be happiest in some sort of outdoor life connected with farming.

'Not a farm, I don't think,' Tara told him.

'But we can go, can't we?' Mandy pleaded. 'We never go anywhere. Everyone else in our class is always going away.'

Allowing for childish exaggeration, Tara knew the criticism was well founded. The twins' school fees meant that there was very little money left over for luxuries such as holidays, although they did spend weekends with her mother and aunt and uncle occasionally. These visits were not always a great success; her mother had never been able to fully conceal her disapproval of the twins' birth, and all the time they were in her company Tara was on tenterhooks in case her mother made some unguarded reference to James.

As disapproving as she had been of Tara herself, it was for James that she had reserved a bitter, intense hatred which had not waned with the years.

And yet in many ways she was more to blame than James, Tara reflected tiredly. By the time she had realised the true nature of her feelings for him it had been too late for her to turn back. Susan's mother was rarely at home; she had a partnership in a business in New York and spent much of her time there, and Tara with adolescent logic, fathoms deep in love, had somehow managed to dismiss her almost entirely from her mind, not attempting to hide her love for James.

With the added wisdom the intervening years had brought Tara could see things more objectively from James' point of view; married to a woman several years his elder, a woman who spent most of her time away from home leaving him alone, a taxing, struggling business to run—was it so very surprising that he had given in to the impulse to take the solace she had so innocently offered?

Perhaps not, but surely he must have known so much better than she had that there was no future for them? Surely he should have had the sophistication and worldly wisdom to call a halt before matters finally got out of hand? That was what she could not forgive him—that he had carelessly disregarded the consequences of allowing a mixture of boredom and sexual desire to overcome the barriers which should have existed between them.

She had been seventeen to his twenty-six—not a

vast difference in terms of years, but in terms of experience . . .

'Mummy, we're here!' Mandy announced shrilly, drawing her attention to the fact that she had been about to drive past the school.

After leaving the twins Tara drove straight to the studio. The moment she walked in she sensed that Chas was in one of his difficult moods. He grunted without looking up from the camera he was engrossed in. A model Tara recognised from previous sessions was sitting tensely on a bentwood chair, the atmosphere in the hot studio thick with tension.

Summing up the situation at a glance, Tara shrugged out of her coat and filled the kettle in the small kitchen attached to the studio. Without saying a word she placed a mug of coffee in front of Chas and went across to chat to the model. She was nineteen, with several successful ad campaigns behind her, and Tara knew from the schedules that she had come in to sit for some practice shots for a *Vogue* feature.

'Is he always like this?' she asked Tara in an agonised whisper. 'I remember last time I came here . . .'

'It's just his way,' Tara soothed her. 'He's an artist with the camera and a perfectionist.'

The other girl grimaced. 'It's at times like these that I wish I'd done as my parents wanted me to and gone on to university!'

Chas's brusque, 'If you two have quite finished on the girl talk, perhaps we can get some work done,' put an end to their conversation.

It was lunchtime before Tara even had time to draw breath. Chas was in the kind of mood where he seemed almost driven, and it was both mentally and physically exhausting trying to keep pace with him.

At two o'clock Chas finally announced irritably that he supposed they ought to break for lunch, and Tara went thankfully to buy them some sandwiches before he changed his mind. It wasn't unusual for him to insist on working right through the day without stopping, and the hungry grumbling of her stomach had been distracting her attention for almost an hour.

When she got back to the studio the model had gone and the phone was ringing. The 'Do not disturb' sign on the darkroom door meant exactly what it said, as she knew from experience, and reaching for the phone she dumped her sandwiches on the table.

The crisp, cool tones of the twins' headmistress sent tremors of fear jangling along her nerves.

'The twins——' she began urgently, but Mrs Ledbetter was obviously used to dealing with anxious parents, because she said soothingly, 'Nothing to worry about, Mrs Bellamy, it's just that Simon has been complaining of stomach ache all morning. Our Matron has checked him over and we can't find anything wrong. He probably just wants a bit of coddling.'

A thin flush of colour ran up under Tara's fine skin as she tried to dissect the calming words to discover if they held an implied rebuke. One of her greatest burdens in bringing up the twins alone was that she couldn't be at home with them. She had never tried to contact James after that first time when Susan's mother had laughed in her face at her naïveté, and there was no one to support the twins apart from herself, so work was a basic necessity. But that didn't stop the guilt, she thought shakily as she hung up, having assured Mrs Ledbetter that she was leaving immediately for the school.

Did every working mother experience this knife-sharp anguish every time her child cried for her and she couldn't be there? Guilt was a burden women seemed fashioned by nature to bear.

Not daring to risk disturbing Chas, she wrote a brief note displaying it prominently on his desk, then hurried outside to her Mini.

Simon was waiting for her in the school's sick bay, looking pale and lethargic. Mandy was with him, and she leaped off her chair and rushed towards Tara, crying importantly, 'Simon's been sick, and he was crying, but I've been looking after him.'

Tara praised her warmly; for all her ebullience and apparent resilience Mandy was still vulnerable, as all children were vulnerable when they lacked the love of one parent.

'I don't think there's really anything much wrong,' Mrs Staines, the Matron assured her with a kind smile. 'A couple of days in bed and some spoiling will probably work wonders.'

A couple of days in bed! Tara groaned, fighting back her dismay. That meant taking two more precious days from her holiday allowance. Chas would be furious. Normally during school holidays she managed to come to an arrangement with a neighbour who lived close to her and who was willing to look after the twins for her, but she was away visiting her parents, and anyway Tara doubted that Simon in his present mood would accept anyone apart from herself.

'Some country air, that will bring the roses back to his cheeks,' Matron pronounced.

'Can we go to the country, Mummy?' Simon pleaded on the way home. He had perked up when he saw her, but he was still listless, and Tara's heart smote her. Poor little scrap; his sickness was no less real for being caused by emotional rather than physical malaise.

'All right,' she gave in, 'but remember, Susan might have changed her mind.'

'She said we could,' Mandy pointed out with irrefutable logic, 'and people should always do things when they say they will.'

Tara suppressed another sigh. Right now she did not feel up to explaining to her daughter the ethics governing adult behaviour, and it sank still further when she reached home to discover Chas's car parked outside.

He saw her drive up and came striding across to the Mini.

'So, how's the wounded soldier?' he asked Simon affably but with narrowed eyes and a certain grimness that alerted Tara's defence mechanisms.

His cool, 'You fuss too much,' as she unlocked the front door and bustled the twins into the kitchen, reinforced her feelings. 'He looks as right as rain to me.'

'Matron said I was to have two days at home,' Simon told Chas informatively. 'Mummy is going to stay with me, and then we're going to spend the weekend in the country.'

'Are you now? Is that true, "Mummy"?' Chas demanded bitterly. 'Funny, but I had the distinct impression that you and I had a date for this weekend.'

'I never promised I would come, Chas,' Tara reminded him. 'As it happens, we've been invited away for the weekend,' she crossed her fingers childishly behind her back, 'and in view of Simon's sickness I feel it would do them both good to get away from London.'

'Really?' Anger kindled in his eyes. 'Now isn't that just a dandy get-out? Well, let me lay it on the line for you, Tara. I want you and you damn well know it. I'm not prepared to play games either.'

Tara felt sick. Here came the crunch; the inevitable catastrophe she had been trying to avoid for weeks.

'Meaning?' she forced herself to say.

'You know what I mean,' Chas replied in a low voice.

'And if I don't agree?'

His answer was simply to glower at her before flinging the door open and striding angrily through it.

She had known it had to come, and Chas's attitude had only reinforced all her own doubts about the feasibility of her continuing to work for him, but she could not deny that giving up her job at this particular minute in time was something she simply could not afford to do.

'Why are you looking like that, Mummy?' Simon demanded suddenly. 'Does your tummy feel funny too?'

'Sort of,' she agreed wryly. 'Now come on, you'd better go and lie down if you aren't feeling well.'

It was early evening when she finally decided to ring Susan to accept her invitation for the weekend. They had nothing to lose by going, Tara decided, and besides, she felt totally unable to cope with the twins' disappointment were she to refuse.

Susan sounded ecstatic when she thanked her for the invitation and accepted it.

'You'll have to give me directions on how to find the place, though,' Tara warned her. 'Where did you say it was?'

'In the Cotswolds,' Susan told her airily. 'But don't worry about getting there. I'll send someone to pick you up if you just tell me what time would be convenient, and give me your address.'

On the point of refusing, Tara remembered the luxurious BMW she had seen outside the school, and contemplated the luxury of being driven in such a vehicle. Susan had mentioned her chauffeur and doubtless this task would be given to him.

They chatted for several minutes, and when Tara mentioned her job Susan was obviously impressed. 'Chas Saunders?' she exclaimed in tones of awe. 'You lucky thing! He's incredibly sexy, isn't he? I've never met him myself, but I've heard about him.'

'Who hasn't?' Tara agreed drily. Chas and his female companion of the moment were popular gossip column fodder.

'You're not involved there yourself, are you?' Susan asked, obviously picking up the undertone in her voice.

Tara's wry, 'Chas is strictly a one-night-stand man,' was an evasive answer, but it seemed to satisfy her friend, who laughed and said teasingly, 'Yeah, but

what a night!' before announcing that she had to go as
she could hear Piers crying.

With the mercurial resilience of children the world
over, Simon declared in the morning that he felt well
enough to return to school and Tara was able to go
back to the studio.

She drove there with mounting dread. Chas was
alone in the huge room when she opened the door. He
looked up, scowled, and then ignored her as she
removed her jacket and hung it on the coat-stand.
They were supposed to be doing some outdoor shots,
so she had dressed comfortably in jeans, and a checked
shirt worn underneath a thick, sleveless sheepskin
waistcoat.

When she had removed her coat she turned round to
find Chas assessing her slim jean-clad body thoughtfully. Despite her resolve colour rose in her cheeks.
She turned away, intending to put the kettle on, but
Chas's 'Tara,' halted her in her tracks.

'Look,' he began irately, 'I'm sorry about yesterday.
I lost my cool, a fatal tactical error.' He grimaced
wryly, running lean fingers through his sun-streaked
fair hair. 'God, I thought I'd learned years ago not to
stampede my prey, but it seems I was wrong. You're
determined to spend this weekend with your friend?'

Dry-mouthed, Tara nodded her head. What was he
going to do? Fire her?

'I know what you're thinking,' he surprised her by
saying in a harsh voice. 'I thought you knew me better
than that. I've never had to apply pressure to get a
woman into bed with me in the past, and I'm damned
well not starting now. I want you, Tara,' he said

frankly, 'but I want you willingly. Sex should be a mutual pleasure, not something to be endured. Why?' he asked helplessly. 'Is it just me who revolts you, or is it men in general? You've been married, had kids—hell . . .'

'I'm sorry, Chas,' Tara broke in quietly. 'And no, it isn't you.' A small smile tugged at her mouth as she remembered how Sue had described him. 'You know better than that,' she teased lightly. 'It's just that you're a one-night-stand man, and I'm a woman with two children dependent on her who . . .'

'Wants the opposite sex to keep its distance from her,' Chas finished astutely for her. 'Even if I offered permanency, it wouldn't make any difference, would it?' he pressed. 'You're still too involved with the guy you married—the twins' father, that's the straight up and down of it, isn't it? For God's sake,' he muttered with suppressed violence, 'when are you going to come out of mourning and realise that life is passing you by? Okay,' he said wearily when he saw the stubborn set of her lips, 'I can see I'm battering my head against a brick wall, but if you ever change your mind . . .'

'You still want me to keep on working with you?' Tara asked shakily.

His eyebrows rose, mockery in the brown eyes. 'Sure I do,' he confirmed. 'It's good for my ego having such a sexy lady about the place, and besides,' he paused and grinned, 'you're the best assistant I've ever had.'

It was with a much lighter heart that Tara went about her work, and she accepted with pleasure when Chas suggested that she take the Friday afternoon off in order to prepare for the weekend away.

'This doesn't mean I've given up,' he warned her, 'simply that I'm declaring a cease-fire, okay?'

She was still smiling when she reached home, even though she was now entertaining grave doubts about the wisdom of agreeing to Sue's invitation. As the Monday was a Bank Holiday Susan had insisted that the three of them stay over for the extra day, and knowing the twins' propensity for getting themselves and their clothes grubby, Tara was kept busy washing and ironing prior to their visit.

Neither of the twins would have much in common with Sue's toddler, she reflected as she packed their cases, but as they prepared for bed on the Friday night, both of them were so excited about the weekend ahead that Tara's heart smote her.

They got so few treats of this nature, it would have been grossly unfair of her to deprive them of it simply because she couldn't face up to the past.

Her mother and James were now divorced, or so Sue had said. What had happened to him? Tara wondered. She had learned from her own mother after the twins' birth that Sue's mother had had a considerable shareholding in the company James had inherited from his father. He had rarely discussed business with her; their time together had been too precious, too highly emotionally charged for Tara to want to waste any of it discussing business.

Forget James, forget the past, she told herself sternly, unwilling to acknowledge the small ache which threatened to flare into agonising pain if she let it. Why had she never been able to free herself from the spell of the past? Other girls suffered similar mishaps and went on to make successful marriages elsewhere; to forge loving relationships with other men—why hadn't she been able to? Was it because she had felt guilty about what had happened? Guilty and besmirched. The attitudes of the small village in which they lived were very narrow, and as well as the burden of James's rejection she had also had to bear the bitter anger of her mother.

If she had not woven such romantic daydreams around James none of it would have happened; but she had refused to see the truth, that he was simply a man trapped in an unhappy marriage who had turned to her for sexual solace and had never for one moment felt a tithe of the love for her that burned within her for him.

# CHAPTER THREE

SHE woke up with a headache; a heavy unrelenting pressure behind her eyes and a lethargic disinclination to do anything, much less spend an entire weekend having to be polite to virtual strangers. But she couldn't disappoint the twins, neither could she run the risk of Chas catching her out in a lie. She wished desperately that he would cease his pursuit of her. In other circumstances she would simply have given him a cool rebuff, but he was her employer and she could not afford to lose her job.

The twins were wildly excited, making her feel guilty about her own dread of the weekend ahead. For some perverse reason Mandy, who normally disdained feminine frills in favour of jeans and sweat-shirts, decided that she wanted to wear a pretty cotton pinafore Tara had bought for her several weeks previously, and by the time the requisite underskirt and spotless white blouse had been found to wear with it Tara's head was thumping nauseously.

Susan had arranged for her chauffuer to pick them up at ten o'clock, and by a miracle by ten to the packing was done and the twins ready, which was more than could be said for her, Tara decided feverishly, tugging a comb through her hair and applying lipstick deftly to the soft curves of her mouth.

The unexpected sunshine had prompted her into a

new outfit she had bought for work and not yet worn. She had seen it in a small boutique off South Moulton Street, reduced because of its small size, and had bought it knowing that it would be just right for the receptions Chas sometimes held in the evening as a publicity exercise.

A rich, vivid blue, it was a three-piece in pure silk with a camisole top which just skimmed the curves of her breasts, and a softly shaped skirt gathered into a deep waistband and topped with a matching jacket, whose sleeves she rolled back in the fashion she had seen adopted by the models who came to the studio.

Working in such an environment meant that she had developed a keen eye for adapting prevalent trends to her own personality. The silk brushed sensuously against her skin; she had left her hair in a soft cloud against her shoulders, and the sample of the new Armarni scent the *Vogue* Beauty Editor had given her had been used to good effect. Such samples were her one and only perk. At Christmas she had been presented with what amounted to almost a full trousseau of luxurious Italian underwear by the manufacturer; a gesture of his gratitude for the effect of advertisements Chas had photographed, although such munificence was relatively rare.

Today she was wearing some of it; the briefest of satin bras trimmed with handmade lace to match the dainty suspender belt and briefs that were part of the set.

Vanity was largely responsible for today's primping, she decided, giving herself a last brief look in her mirror. Even though at one time she and Susan had once been as close as sisters a wide gulf yawned between them now.

Susan was a rich man's wife, and it showed, and although she would never be guilty of patronising a less fortunate friend, Tara had no wish to earn her pity by arriving in inexpensive chain-store casuals.

First impressions always counted, Tara reminded herself and when she and the twins stepped out of Susan's Rolls she didn't want them to look like the poor relations.

Susan had explained to her that she and her husband would be driving down to the country ahead of them, which was why the Rolls was free to transport Tara, but despite the knowledge that her appearance was both chic and sophisticated she couldn't stop the tiny bubbles of anxiety forming in the pit of her stomach when the twins' joint shrieks announced the arrival of their transport.

Not wanting to keep the chauffeur waiting, Tara sped downstairs, picking up their case with one hand and ushering the twins through the front door with the other. Outside she told them to wait while she checked her handbag for keys and money, and carefully locked the door.

The sight of the immaculate Rolls seemed to have a subduing effect upon the twins, because they clung uncertainly to Tara's side as she hustled them towards the waiting car.

As they approached it the driver's door opened and a man emerged. Her first thought was that he wasn't wearing a uniform, but this was quickly submerged by a sickening wave of recognition mingled with stunned disbelief.

'Tara!'

He said her name evenly, the inflection which in the past had sent her weak-kneed with pleasure totally banished. He had changed; or was it simply that her perception of him had changed from that of a bemused teenager to that of a disillusioned woman?

'James.' Somehow she managed to force a stiff smile from features as tautly fragile as eggshells. Now she was the one clinging to the twins, filled by an overwhelming impulse to turn on her heel and seek the sanctuary of her home.

James barely glanced at his children, and watching his cool disregard of them, Tara forced back an hysterical impulse to laugh. So much for all those daydreams she had woven during the long lonely months of her pregnancy when she had fantasised about James appearing to discover that she was the mother of his child and being overcome by love for both of them.

'Quite a surprise,' she managed to say calmly. 'Susan never mentioned that you would be picking us up.'

'A last-minute arrangement,' James told her briefly without looking at her. 'I've just returned from the States and when I invited myself down to Dovecote for the weekend they suggested that I give you a lift so that they could give their chauffeur a weekend off.'

'Susan should have telephoned, I could have used my own car.'

Tara flushed when his eyes suddenly fastened on her face; no longer the warm, teasing dark blue she remembered but as hard and flat as river pebbles and totally without expression as they surveyed her heightened colour and defensive grip on the twins.

'Mummy, you're hurting me!' Mandy protested, casting an upward glance at the tall, dark-haired man watching them; a glance which Tara noticed was full of coquettishly innocent appeal.

'Why don't we all get in the car!' James suggested, bending to relieve Tara of the weight of the case. Their fingers touched accidentally, and Tara withdrew as though she had been burned by live coals.

'Explicit but unnecessary,' James told her crisply, stowing her case away, 'I got the message the first time round.'

Tara assumed that he was referring to the shock which must have been apparent when she saw him step out of the car. This meeting must be as unwelcome to him as it was to her, she reflected miserably as she followed the children to the waiting car, but at least he had had the advantage of being forearmed.

The first ten minutes of their journey passed easily enough as the twins exclaimed over the luxury of their transport; Tara couldn't help wishing that James had not ushered her into the front passenger seat, but it seemed gauche to make a fuss about it. After all, he could scarcely have any more desire for her company than she had for his!

He was both the same and yet different, she decided, stealing a brief glance at his impassive profile. There was a total and unrelenting male hardness about him now that she did not remember; when she was seventeen he had seemed the epitome of all her adolescent dreams; gentle, understanding, tender. No one would ever dream of attributing those virtues to the man now seated next to her.

His dark hair was still untouched by grey; and although he was wearing a discreetly expensive suit she suspected that physically he had changed little in the seven years they had been apart. There had been a supple arrogance about the way he had walked towards her which suggested that he was a man at the peak of physical perfection. She remembered the cataclysmic night he had returned from California; then his skin had had the silky sheen of a sun tan, his body a rich bronze. Her palms tingled as though she could still feel the soft suppleness of his flesh against them, and she shuddered deeply, wrenching her thoughts away from the past.

In the back seat the twins were playing a game, vying with one another in their attempts to count as many cars of a particular type as they could.

'Susan tells me you're a widow.'

He hadn't taken his eyes off the road. Tara felt as though a huge boulder were stuck in her throat.

'Yes,' she agreed, forcing out the lie.

'I'm sorry.' The words were a formality. 'What happened?'

'John was killed abroad,' Tara said huskily, repeating the fabrication which had become familiar to her over the years. 'Before the twins were born. They never knew him, nor he them.'

'A mutual loss,' James said quietly. 'You've never thought of remarrying?'

'One has to be asked,' Tara heard herself saying drily, to her own surprise. 'Besides,' she moved restlessly in her deep hide-covered seat, 'I believe one parent who really cares is more important than two who quarrel.'

'You yourself lost your father, if I remember rightly,' James commented. 'At least with your own experience to call upon you'll be able to ensure that your own daughter doesn't fall into the same traps.'

'People normally make their own mistakes,' Tara said tiredly. Although the comment had been delivered in a perfectly flat emotionless voice she had been vividly reminded of one occasion when they had been together and he had accused her of trying to turn him into a father-substitute. She had been furious, reminding him that it was eight years that separated them, not eighteen.

'You've been working in America?' she asked him, deliberately trying to change the subject.

'I have various business interests there, some jointly with Susan's mother. Susan will have told you that she's married again?'

'Yes. Actually I didn't realise . . .' Tara broke off and moistened her suddenly dry lips. She had been going to say that the had not realised they were divorced, but the remark had provocative undertones she wanted to avoid.

'That Hilary would venture into marriage again?' He shrugged. 'Like many women of her wealth and generation she tends to make a career of it. This one's number four.'

'Four!' It was too late for her to hide her surprise. As far as she knew James had been Hilary's second husband.

'You sound surprised?'

'I hadn't realised you'd been divorced long enough for her to have remarried twice. I . . .'

'You didn't stay around long enough to find out.'

The cool comment nonplussed her. It was almost an accusation, but what did James possibly have to accuse her about? He had been the one who had rejected her; who had laughed with Hilary about her foolish love for him, and who had coldly turned his back on her, leaving her to face the trauma of the twins' birth alone.

'What was I supposed to do?' she asked in a bitter, low voice. 'I couldn't put the clock back, I . . .'

'So you scuttled off into a nice, safe marriage?'

Colour burned along her cheekbones, her fingernails digging into the palms of her hands. She would never, never have agreed to this weekend if she had had the slightest suspicion that James was going to be there. How on earth was she going to endure it? Especially if he was going to keep taunting her with these barbed remarks.

Simon distracted her attention excitedly, pointing out some sheep grazing in a field. They had turned on to the M4 and were travelling west.

To Tara's surprise, just after twelve James pulled off the motorway and took a minor road which wound its way down a narrow B-road bordered by high hedges laced with early summer flowers.

'I told Sue that I'd give you lunch,' he explained, answering Tara's unspoken question. 'The house is a large one and although she does have some help she and Alec go down there primarily to relax.'

Before Tara could object he turned into an immaculate drive, marked 'Country Club—members only.'

'Relax,' she was instructed. 'I'm a member and they've been warned to expect us. I own a house locally myself, although at the moment it's occupied by some American friends of mine.'

The country club had once been a farmhouse and the large barn had been converted into an attractive restaurant with high oriel windows set along the length of it and a separate bar inside which occupied a galleried landing.

The twins were entranced, as much by the novelty of eating out as by their surroundings. Mandy gravely confided to James, as she attached herself to his side, that it was just as well she had worn her best dress.

The comment invited a response, and Tara's unwary heart lurched when James bent his head equally gravely and said, 'You look very pretty in it. Blue suits you.'

'Mummy chose it,' Mandy informed him, visibly expanding. 'I normally wear jeans 'cos they're more fun to play in. Have you got any children?' she asked him forthrightly. She was at that stage when the niceties of curbing personal questions were ignored and seemed to have developed a thirst for knowledge about other people's private lives.

'Mandy . . .' Tara warned, but James silenced her, lifting his eyebrows and saying smoothly. 'Regrettably, no.'

Hypocrite, Tara thought resentfully as they were escorted to a table. He didn't want any children, any responsibility for lives other than his own.

However, despite his lack of parental experience he was very adroit at ordering suitable food for the twins and keeping them occupied while they waited for their meal to arrive. Like Tara herself, their school believed strongly in the importance of good manners, and Tara felt a small thrill of pride at the way Simon and

Mandy adapted to their surroundings. They were drawing admiring smiles from other diners, and one woman en route to her table stopped off to speak to James, whom she obviously knew, staring rather hard at Tara and the twins.

'Margot, let me introduce Tara and the twins to you. Tara is an old schoolfriend of Sue's. Margot is one of Sue's neighbours,' James explained. 'Like you, she's a widow.'

'Only I don't have any children, darling,' the other woman pointed out, eyeing the twins unfavourably.

She was somewhere in her late thirties, Tara estimated, although she concealed the fact well, but in her job Tara had become adept at judging what lay beneath the most skilfully applied make-up. She was also subtly warning her that James was strictly private property, Tara acknowledged. She could have him, she thought vehemently, pushing away her sweet untouched and refusing to acknowledge the swiftly stabbing pain their relationship brought, and dismissing the nauseous feeling in her stomach as the result of too much to eat.

Watching the waiter's deferential attitude towards James, Tara was vividly reminded of the one and only occasion they had dined out together. It had been Sue's fifteenth birthday; and she had been dizzy with delight when he announced that he had booked a table at a locally acclaimed restaurant. Even the knowledge that Sue was to accompany them had done nothing to dissipate her mother's disapproval, Tara remembered. She also remembered the brief kiss James had pressed on her untried lips before pushing her out of the car when he took her home. That kiss had changed everything between them.

'Physically the twins aren't like you at all.' James's cool observation cut across the disturbing memories of the past. 'They must take after their father.'

Her fork clattered noisily on to the floor as an abrupt movement dislodged it. Her face the colour of the tablecloth, Tara bent to retrieve it, glad of the opportunity to escape James's too seeing eyes.

'Do they?'

Was he blind? she wondered hysterically. Could he really not see in the twins' features the many resemblances to himself that struck her every day?

'Strange,' he mused, frowning a little. 'They remind me of someone.'

Tara thought her heart would stop beating, but somehow she managed to shrug noncommittally, turning away to urge the children to finish their meal.

'Did I know him?' There was a terse urgency in the question that caught her off guard.

'I . . .'

'You met him when you went to stay with your aunt and uncle, or so I heard in the village. It must have been a whirlwind courtship,' he sneered, glancing meaningfully at the twins. 'Or did you afford him the same privileges I once thought belonged exclusively to me?'

If they hadn't been in public there was no way she could have prevented herself from hitting him. As it was, it was only by a supreme effort of will that she was able to prevent herself from screaming the truth at him.

With that one sentence he had managed to destroy the last fragile, lingering remnants of her romantic daydreams; beliefs she had clung to without even being aware that she was doing so. His words forced her to admit that what for her had been the experience of a lifetime had for him been nothing more than the gratification of momentary lust, otherwise he could never have spoken to her as he just had.

From somewhere she mustered the dignity to say calmly, 'The personal relationship I enjoyed with the twins' father is something very precious to me, and I don't discuss it with anyone.'

'Including your children,' James pointed out astutely. 'I don't think I've heard them mention him once. Did you love him so much that you can't even bear to share his memory with his children? You did love him, I suppose? Unless my memory deceives me you were an extremely sensual creature; hot-blooded, shall we say,' he added drily, his mouth twisting, 'but with a certain prudishness curiously at odds with your real personality. I suppose in those circumstances it wouldn't have been impossible for you to marry young; to legalise those desires of which your mother had taught you to be so ashamed.'

Tara was relieved that the twins were too engrossed in their own conversation and their surroundings to pay any attention to them. Where her face had been pale, now it was hotly flushed, words of bitter denial trembling on her lips, but all she could manage was a fierce, choked, 'I did love him, and you have no right to say such things!'

'No right?' His laughter was bitterly harsh. 'How can you say that, when . . .' He broke off as Mandy suddenly claimed his attention, and not wanting to prolong the conversation, Tara hustled both children

out of their seats, saying feverishly that it was time they
were on their way.

James unlocked the car and made sure the twins
were comfortable in the back, but when Tara would
have joined them he forestalled her again, firmly
closing the door and then reaching past her to unlock
the passenger door.

His arm brushed against the thin silk of her jacket
and she froze, as physically aware of the hardness of
his flesh as she would have been had their contact
been skin upon skin. She always had been acutely
aware of him, and that at least had not changed. He
was a disturbingly sensual man and her body, no
longer that of a girl, naïve about the opposite sex,
responded instinctively to him, the bones in her skull
clenching against the knowledge of her vulnerability to
him. Being close to him was like losing a toughened
outer layer of skin; a physically painful process leaving
nerve endings far too close to the surface and every
one of them reacting to his proximity. Even so, she
refused to move away, telling herself that to do so
would be stupidly selfconscious, but all her hard-
learned composure was not enough to slow the hurried
thudding of her heart or stop the aching tension of her
throat.

His fingers gripped the door handle; lean and
brown, a discreet sheen of gold at his cuff, the
immaculate shirt protruding exactly half an inch below
the expensive wool of his suit jacket. The door opened
and his free hand was on her elbow; an automatic
gesture of assistance, and yet somehow Tara sensed
that it had been deliberate, although it was impossible
to know why, especially when, risking an upward

glance into his face, she surprised upon it a look of acute dislike, reinforced by the swiftness with which his hand was withdrawn.

At best she should have felt nothing; at worst relief, but instead what she did feel was a bleak and terrifying sense of rejection.

Old habits died hard, she told herself cynically as he closed the door on her and walked round the front of the car; and somehow she had never recovered from the habit of being rejected by James.

Her flesh still tingled where he had touched it, and although the twins were soon drowsy and on the verge of sleep, Tara herself found it almost impossible to relax.

It was a relief when the Rolls finally turned into the cobbled forecourt of what James explained to her had once been a Cotswold farmhouse. Now the cream stone was weathered with age, and early flowering pale yellow roses smothered the front south-facing wall.

The farmhouse, although large and rambling, had a comfortable, welcoming ambience that helped to soothe a little of Tara's taut anxiety, especially when Sue came hurrying out to greet them the moment she heard the Rolls. James and Tara were hugged unceremoniously. 'This is lovely!' Sue exclaimed with genuine warmth as she led them inside.

A copper bowl full of the same roses Tara had seen outside gleamed on a polished mahogany table. The hall was square with warm panelling and a parquet floor. An intricately carved banister curved upwards and out of sight, a tall window on the half landing flooding the hall with light and trapping dusty motes in its golden gleam.

A cream labrador had materialised from outside, throughly enjoying the fuss the twins were making of her. Firmly detaching them, Tara followed Sue towards the stairs.

'I'll just show you to your rooms and then we'll have a cup of tea and a chat. Oh, it's all right,' she smiled when she saw the twins' disappointed faces. 'We don't stand on ceremony down here, and although Alec tends to disapprove Misty is allowed upstairs.'

'Where is Alec?' James asked.

'In the study. He had to bring some work up with him. I think he'll appreciate a helping hand. Alec manages one of James's companies,' Sue explained to Tara with a grin. 'That's how I met him.' She grimaced as a thin childish cry pierced the warmth of the afternoon. 'There's Piers—furious! I put him down for a sleep after lunch. It's a miracle he's slept this long really. I keep telling myself it's time we provided him with a brother or sister—at the moment he tends to be the centre of attention and he knows it. Remember,' she commented to Tara taking the next flight of stairs, 'how we used to say that neither of us would settle for just one child after our own experiences?' She laughed. 'I knew you meant it, but I didn't guess how you were going to achieve it!'

'I've put the twins next to you,' she added. 'The rooms have a connecting door. Oh, and by the way, the plumbing arrangements are somewhat archaic as yet, so you and James will be sharing a bathroom. I hope you don't mind?'

'She doesn't mean literally,' James murmured jokingly, so that only Tara could hear, adding, 'Don't worry, you're quite safe. I've reached the age where I restrict my indulgence in water sports to swimming and sailing.'

'You're in your normal room, James,' Sue told him as they reached the landing. 'And these are your rooms,' she told Tara, pausing outside a heavy oak door. 'This part of the house was once the barn, but it's been converted into living space.'

James had disappeared, into his own room, Tara presumed, and she felt free to echo Mandy's sigh of pleasure when Sue opened the door to reveal an attractive bedroom with open beams and a tiny mullioned window.

'We've tried to keep as much of the country atmosphere as possible without being too earnestly authentic,' she explained.

'It's lovely!' Tara enthused admiringly. The room was decorated in pastels and soft greens; pretty fresh cotton curtains at the windows and a traditional American patchwork quilt on the bed.

'James brought that back from one of his trips,' Sue told her. 'Do you find him very changed?'

'A little older,' Tara said cautiously.

'I was thrilled when he called to say he was back in England. We don't see as much of him as we'd like— the companies take up most of his time. It's funny really, in many ways he means more to me than my mother, although he's scarcely the traditional father figure.'

'You must have been very sorry when their marriage broke up,' Tara said, hoping that her voice wouldn't betray her.

Sue shrugged. 'Not really. I could never understand

why James married my mother.' She frowned. 'There was always something odd about it, and not just because he was younger than her. You know, when I look back I can't believe that he ever loved her or that she loved him.'

'There are other reasons for marriage,' Tara said emotionlessly.

'I know, but somehow I could never imagine James marrying without a deep emotional commitment—he just doesn't strike me as that kind of man. Look, I'll go downstairs and ask Mrs B., our treasure, to make us a pot of tea and some orange for the kids, and you come down when you're ready and I'll introduce you to Alec. We'll be in the sitting room. It looks out over the gardens, first left in the hall.' She walked towards the door, paused and then said impulsively, 'I'm so glad you and James could both be here together. It's almost like old times . . .'

They viewed 'old times' differently, Tara thought tiredly as she unpacked for the twins and herself; Simon and Mandy had made themselves at home almost immediately, and within twenty minutes of Sue leaving them they were ready to return downstairs with Tara; their hands and faces washed and the clothes they had travelled in exchanged for dungarees and tee-shirts.

Everyone else was already in the sitting room, as Sue had called it, but what in actual fact was a generously proportioned room furnished in tones of pale lemon and soft blue, with huge french windows opening on to the gardens.

Misty the dog fanned her tail gently on the floor when she saw the twins. Simon beamed with pleasure, twisting round to tell Tara in hushed tones, 'I think she likes me.'

Alec, Sue's husband, turned out to be a pleasant, sturdy-looking individual in his late twenties, obviously devoted to his more effervescent wife. He greeted Tara enthusiastically, telling her with a smile that he had heard a good deal about her from Sue over the years.

'I always regretted losing touch with you,' Sue added. 'I couldn't believe it when I came back from that duty holiday in New York with my mother to find you'd left the village, and then when your mother told me you'd married . . .'

'You're a widow, Sue tells me,' Alec continued, his smile sympathetic.

Feeling a dreadful fraud, Tara nodded.

'It can't have been easy for you.'

Again that quiet sympathy.

'I've been lucky,' she replied huskily. 'Especially in my job.'

'You work for Chas Saunders the photographer, so Sue says.' James interrupted.

His tone rather than his words made Tara flush. She was well aware of the reputation Chas had, the number of affairs he was reputed to have indulged in, and she could tell without him putting it into words that James suspected she was one of the many strings to Chas's bow.

'You must lead a very glamorous life,' Sue commented with a trace of envy, 'mixing with models and celebrities.'

'I don't know so much about "glamorous"; it's certainly hard work,' Tara told her ruefully, accepting a cup of tea. Mandy was crouching on the floor, distracting the attention of young Master Piers, who had been busily engrossed in unravelling the thread sewing a small motif to his velour jumpsuit, while Simon was quite happy stroking Misty.

Alec and James resumed the conversation they had obviously been having before her entry, and Tara grimaced a little when Sue said softly, 'You've got two great kids there, Tara. It must have been terribly hard for you—and them. I can remember exactly how it felt only having one parent.'

'Yes, I worry about it sometimes,' Tara admitted. 'You know,' she pulled a face, 'all the usual things—is Simon being deprived of a masculine influence to pattern himself on; are both of them suffering emotionally from the lack of a father and the fact that I have to work.'

'You know even now, I can hardly believe it,' Sue marvelled. 'I never thought you'd marry impetuously like that. You always used to talk about having a career and . . .'

'Girls of seventeen are notorious for changing their minds when they fall in love,' James commented sardonically behind them, making Tara start. She hadn't realised he was listening to their conversation and covered her momentary confusion by saying evenly, and truthfully, 'Having the twins is something I've never regretted.'

Mandy was trying to pick up Piers, her small features compressed with the effort.

'Do you know, she does remind me of someone,' Sue murmured. 'What do you think, Alec?' she appealed to her husband.

He studied Mandy for a moment and then shook his head. 'Probably a similarity of expression that she shares with Tara.'

'Mm, but neither of them look like Tara . . .'

'We look like our daddy,' Mandy said importantly, deciding it was time she joined the conversation. 'Mummy told us that when we were little.'

'So you do talk to them about their father,' James commented sotto voce.

'Sue, I wonder would you mind if we went upstairs to rest for a while?' Tara asked her hostess, ignoring James's taunt. 'I'm afraid I've got a headache, and . . .'

'Of course you can,' Sue interrupted before she could finish. 'You poor thing! I remember those terrible headaches you used to get. But don't worry about the twins—they can stay down here. Mrs B. normally organises a nursery tea for six, although we don't normally eat until about eight.' She glanced at her watch. 'It's four now, so you've got three hours before you need to do anything.'

Feeling terrible, Tara started to protest, but Sue overruled her. 'It's not an imposition,' she corrected firmly. 'I'm dying to get the twins to myself; I can see Mandy is going to be a treasure where Piers is concerned, and Simon can help by taking Misty for her tea-time walk.'

Knowing when she was defeated, Tara thanked her again and headed for her room. Once there she stripped off her suit and pulled on a thin wrap before curling up on the large double bed. She had taken a couple of her headache tablets and as they started to take effect her drowsy mind became full of memories of the past, of James, and as she hovered in the

twilight world between waking and sleeping she felt
the present slip away from her and she was once again
seventeen, on the brink of love and womanhood.

# CHAPTER FOUR

'AND you will stay the night with me, won't you, Tara? If you don't I'll be all on my own, and you promised you'd help me with my maths.'

Tara grinned down at the earnest fourteen-year-old face. If she was honest with herself she would admit that in many ways she preferred Susan's home to her own; for one thing it was always warm and for another they could spread their school books out without incurring any of the harsh criticism such behaviour normally invoked from her own mother.

Tara suppressed a small sigh as she thought of her mother. Aunt Mary had once told her that her mother had been a pretty and popular girl before her marriage, but Tara found that hard to accept now, and during her last visit she had heard her aunt commenting in an undertone to her mother that she was too hard on her. It wasn't fair, Tara reflected rebelliously. On the one hand her mother refused to allow her out to parties or the cinema with the other girls from school, telling her that if she wanted to make anything of herself she would have to work hard so that she could get good A level passes and go on to university, and yet when she tried to study Tara invariably found that her mother had a dozen or more small jobs for her to do, all accompanied by muttered grumblings about the untidiness and laziness of teenage girls.

She and her mother had never been close. Tara did have a very dim memory of the days when her father was alive, when their small house had seemed a happier, warmer place, but he had died over ten years ago and althouth there had been sufficient insurance to keep Tara and her mother in modest comfort there was no extra for the luxuries she had seen in Susan's home.

'You are coming, aren't you?'

'I promised I would, didn't I? Of course I'm coming,' she told her.

Some of Tara's classmates were scornful of the friendship which had sprung up between Tara and the three years younger Susan, but for all her lack of years Susan had a worldliness that bridged the age gap and sometimes made Tara's heart ache for the loneliness concealed behind the air of defiance.

'I'll see you at four, then,' Susan announced, jumping up from her sitting position on the floor at Tara's side as the bell signalling the end of the lunch break went.

'I thought third-formers weren't allowed in these studies,' one of Tara's classmates commented caustically, entering the room as Susan left. 'Honestly, Tara, you shouldn't encourage her, spoiled little brat! Mummy wanted to send her to boarding school, but she's been expelled from so many she couldn't find one to take her. God, what I wouldn't give to have rich parents,' she groaned, rolling her eyes theatrically. 'No more school for me!'

For all the scorn some of the girls heaped on Susan's head, there were very few of them who weren't secretly impressed by her mother's wealth.

Hilary Harvey had become a legend in the few short months she had lived in Hillingdon. She had bought what had once been the local Manor House and spent literally thousands on modernising it. Interior decorators had come down from London; a kitchen such as most of the inhabitants of Hillingdon had only seen on American soap operas had been installed, together with several luxurious bathrooms.

Tara had been unwillingly impressed when Susan had shown her round, but, sensible beyond her years, she had sensed loneliness and uncertainty beneath Susan's apparent gloating manner, and so she had pushed aside any feelings of jealousy and concentrated on finding the real Susan, hidden away behind the defensive barricades.

'God knows why you should want to be friends with her anyway,' her classmate commented in disgust. 'You've always been such a goody two-shoes, and for all that she's only fourteen I've heard . . .'

'I'm not interested in what you've heard, Jill,' Tara cut in quietly. 'It's only gossip anyway.'

Malice gleamed in the other girl's pale blue eyes. Tara had never run with the crowd and kept herself slightly aloof from the giggles and whispered confidences concerning boy-friends and dates which were bandied about between the other girls during free periods and lunch breaks, and this, coupled with her intelligence and faint air of disdain, had generated jealousy among some of the girls, including Jill Blady.

'Huh, Miss High and Mighty,' Jill interrupted bitterly, 'but not too high and mighty to make friends with the richest girl in the neighbourhood, even if she is three years younger than you and nothing but a little tart!'

Before Tara could retort she had slammed out of the study, leaving Tara alone. She managed to put the unpleasant incident out of her mind during the afternoon. English literature was one of her favourite lessons and it was easy to lose herself among the heady pleasure of Shakespeare's Sonnets.

At four o'clock when she went to collect her bicycle from the shed she found Susan waiting for her, her expression so wary and uncertain that she forced herself to put Jill's envious comments out of her mind and concentrate instead on the younger girl. Was she really thought of as a 'goody-goody' by her peers? she wondered uncertainly as they cycled leisurely down the country lane which led to Susan's home. It was an unpleasant thought, and one that made her want to examine her own motives for befriending Susan more deeply. It was true that they were divided by age and culture, and yet there was something about Susan, an air of aloneness, that called to something within herself.

'You're not listening,' Susan protested. 'My father's coming home soon. You'll love him, Tara.'

Tara hadn't met Susan's father, although she had heard a lot about him. Susan adored him and talked of him constantly. Tara had built up the impression of a kindly, indulgent man who was no match for his aggressive, domineering wife.

'Is your mother coming back as well?' Tara asked unenthusiastically. She had only met Susan's mother once and had gained the distinct impression that Hilary Harvey hadn't liked her; an impression which was confirmed when Susan had confided artlessly that her mother generally disliked all her friends.

The Manor House had been built during the reign of Queen Anne and the mellow late afternoon spring sun bathed the front of the building in a golden glow. Tara, always acutely sensitive to moods and surroundings, felt touched by a nostalgia she could barely understand as she brought her cycle to a halt several yards from the house.

'Come on,' Susan called, less attuned to the golden perfection of the afternoon. 'I'm hungry!'

A housekeeper looked after the house in Susan's mother's absence; providing meals and a watchful eye, although it was far less strict than Tara's mother's, and Tara was often slightly shocked by the amount of freedom Susan was allowed.

Even now she felt a little surprised by the ease with which she had been able to persuade her mother to allow her to stay overnight with Susan.

When they had first met Susan had talked glibly of the sophisticated life she had led with her mother, but once she had realised that Tara wasn't impressed by her tales of wild parties at her Swiss boarding school, of the drinks and drugs indulged in by the teenage set in which she claimed to move, Susan had swiftly dropped her pseudo-sophisticated image.

Mrs Lear, the housekeeper, expressed relief when she saw that Tara was with Susan.

'It's my daughter,' she explained briefly. 'Her husband rang me a few hours ago. Gayle has started the baby and Jonathan wants to stay with little Peter while he's at the hospital. I didn't want to leave Miss Susan on her own, but if you're staying overnight . . .'

'We'll be fine,' Tara assured her. 'You go to your

daughter, Mrs Lear, don't worry about us.'

When Mrs Lear had gone Tara briskly set about preparing an omelette for their evening meal, watched by Susan with undisguised awe.

'Grief!' she exclaimed watching Tara's expertise. 'I can't even boil an egg.'

'You're going to have to find a rich husband, then,' Tara teased, 'or hasn't your mother told you yet that the best way to a man's heart is through his stomach?'

'My mother believes that the best way to get a man is to buy him,' Susan retorted cynically, the bitter expression on her young face shocking Tara into silence. She had heard rumours in the small town about Susan's mother, but had naïvely dismissed them as mere gossip. What was Susan implying? That her mother was unfaithful to her father? No one apart from Susan seemed to mention Mr Harvey. Susan's mother was the one who controlled the family reins. Susan had once told her that her mother had been left a lot of money by her parents and that this money was invested in various businesses in America, where Susan's grandparents had lived. But what of Susan's father? What did he do for a living? Susan had said vaguely once that he was abroad 'working', and knowing how sensitive she was on the subject of her parents Tara had been reluctant to pry. Susan was fiercely defensive of her father, but privately Tara suspected he was too gentle and weak to stand up to his strong-willed wife, even to protect his child. She knew it was wrong of her, but she tended to despise him a little. Couldn't he see that Susan needed him?

This thought was very much uppermost in Tara's mind when she undressed for bed in the room next to

Susan's. As she had discovered during previous visits to the Manor House, Susan suffered from frightening nightmares, often crying out in the night for her father, although in the morning she appeared to remember nothing of them.

She didn't know which was worse, Tara mused as she slid in between the expensive pure cotton sheets—having a father one rarely saw, or being deprived of one altogether as she had been.

She fell into a light sleep from which she woke abruptly, ears straining in the heavy silence without knowing what she was listening for.

It was the dryness of her throat that prompted her to go downstairs to the kitchen in search of a cooling drink. She knew the house well enough not to need to switch on any lights. The kitchen door was ajar and she pushed it open, automatically flinching as her bare feet came into contact with the icy cold ceramic floor tiles. She was just about to turn on the cold tap when the atavistic prickling of the tiny hairs on her arms warned her that she wasn't alone. She swung round in panic at the precise moment that strong fingers gripped her bare upper arms, warm male breath brushing her hair as an incredulous voice proclaimed softly, 'Sue?'

Responding automatically, Tara stammered, 'Sue's in bed. I'm her friend Tara . . .'

'Lord, yes,' the husky voice continued tiredly. 'She mentioned you in her last letter.' Her arms were released and Tara saw his bulky shadow move as he reached for the light switch.

As the harsh brilliance flooded the kitchen she blinked hazily, forgetting the transparency of her thin cotton nightdress—a year old and almost outgrown, the thin fabric stretched tight across the taut swell of her high breasts. When she opened her eyes she reeled in shock, recognising even in her naïvety and inexperience the potent masculinity of the man standing opposite her. Tiredness did nothing to detract from the lean suppleness of his six-foot-odd frame, a thin black polo-necked wool sweater clinging to the powerful muscles of his shoulders and chest, narrow black trousers revealing the taut thrust of male hipbones and thighs. Against her will Tara's gaze returned to his face, and her eyes rounded with surprise as they recognised the smouldering sensual appeal of dark blue eyes and the dangerous attraction of the hardboned, totally male face in which they were set.

'Who . . . who are you?' she demanded hesitantly at last, striving to hang on to her dignity and the responsibility Mrs Lear had thrust upon her shoulders. The hideous possibility that this man might be some undesirable acquaintance of whom Susan's mother would undoubtedly disapprove could not be ignored. One glance had been sufficient to convince her that this man, whoever he was, was no fit companion for a fourteen-year-old girl. He bore all the signs of experience and cynicism which even Tara recognised as being a lethal and highly explosive mixture, and yet despite her revealing attire there was nothing in the icy blue eyes to make her feel uncomfortable as they skimmed quickly over her pale worried face and slender, coltish body.

'Where's Mrs Lear?' he demanded calmly, ignoring Tara's question, indifference giving way to anger as her expression betrayed her and he exhaled smokily, his eyes darkening. 'Don't tell me Hilary's left Sue in this barn of a place with no one but another schoolgirl for company?'

'Mrs Lear had to leave unexpectedly,' Tara told him hurriedly, recognising instinctively the tone of authority in his voice and wanting to protect the housekeeper. 'How did you get in? The doors were locked—I checked myself.'

'And now you're looking at me as though I were Lucifer himself,' he mocked softly. 'I'm sorry to disappoint you. Nothing so dramatic. I used this.' He produced a key, and grimaced suddenly, flexing his shoulders. 'God, I'm tired! Transatlantic flights are a refined form of torture. There wouldn't happen to be any milk in the fridge, would there?' When Tara nodded he dropped wearily into a chair, legs stretched out in front of him, leaning backwards eyes slightly closed, hands clasped loosely in front of him. 'Be a good girl and pour me a glass,' he said softly without moving.

Compelled by a will stronger than her own, Tara did as he demanded, and placed the glass in front of him on the table.

'It's all right, I don't bite,' he told her sardonically, making her jump as she pushed the glass hesitantly towards him, and she wondered how he had known she was nervous when his eyes were closed.

'How is Sue?' he asked when he had drained the glass. 'She's had a rough time recently, poor kid. Hilary isn't the best of mothers. No comment?' he said wryly. 'Tactful but unnecessary. Hilary herself makes no secret of the fact that she finds motherhood an unwanted chore. Now why are you looking at me like that?' Suddenly the blue eyes were open, watching her with an unwavering glance that was acutely perceptive.

'I'll get you something to eat,' Tara heard herself saying nervously. 'You must be hungry. Travelling always makes me feel hungry.' She was babbling nonsense, but she couldn't seem to stop, her eyes constantly avoiding those searching blue ones as she bustled about the kitchen.

'Okay, I can understand why you don't want to discuss Sue's mother—but there's more to it than that, isn't there?' her companion continued perceptively, leaning across to take the carton of eggs Tara had removed from the fridge from her suddenly nerveless fingers. His hands were warm and hard, his fingers lean, the nails clean and well manicured. She found herself studying them in helpless fascination, strange, unnerving emotions stirred into life as she imagined those fingers against her skin, touching her . . . She shuddered violently and pulled away, appalled by the direction of her thoughts, shocked by their unwanted sensuality and the fear that this stranger might read it in her eyes.

'What's the matter?' he drawled sardonically. 'Cat got your tongue?'

'Sue has two parents,' Tara retorted unwisely, breaking the eggs neatly into a bowl. A mother *and* a father,' she emphasised,

'And?' One dark eyebrow rose interrogatively, the blue eyes narrowed; concentrating on her face, suddenly steely.

'And . . .' Heavens, why did she feel like this, so

awkward and clumsy, lost for words in front of this intimidating man?

'And she misses her father,' Tara said huskily at last. 'She misses him and loves him, and he must know what her mother is doing to her, but he makes no effort to intervene.'

'Go on . . .' She had captured his attention now and the blue eyes had hardened. Her courage deserted her. She swallowed, wishing she had never spoken.

'You were saying,' the hard voice continued, 'Sue misses her f . .' he paused and then finished smoothly, 'her father. You have a very revealing face, Tara, and it tells me that you don't altogether approve of Sue's father.'

'She needs him,' Tara said quietly, 'but he's never here. He lets her mother bully and hurt her. Oh, I don't suppose he can help it,' she added quickly. 'It can't be easy for a gentle-natured man to stand up to someone like Mrs . . .' Her voice faded gently and she bit down hard on the tremulous softness of her lip, wishing she had never allowed herself to be dragged into this conversation.

'Is that how Sue describes her father?' Tara's companion asked in an odd tone. 'As weak and uncaring?'

Once more Tara's expression betrayed her, and a vivid flush stained her skin, making it unnecessary for her to admit that she had drawn her own conclusions from Sue's adoring remarks about the father who seemed to have so little time to spend with her.

'Sue loves him very much,' she murmured haltingly. 'I'd better go back to her. Who shall I say?' She was remembering suddenly the key he had shown her.

He smiled sardonically, replacing the empty glass and getting to his feet. 'Sorry, I'm forgetting the formalities, aren't I? I haven't introduced myself. James Harvey,' he told her briefly, watching the realisation dawning in her eyes. 'That's right,' he told her softly. 'Sue's weak uncaring father—or rather stepfather. Didn't it ever occur to you when you were jumping to all those rash decisions that stepfathers have to tread very warily with children who aren't legally theirs?'

Stepfather! He was Sue's stepfather! A mass of conflicting emotions seized her, paramount among which was a sense of sick disbelief that this man could actually be married to Sue's mother, combined with a bitter chagrin that she had been stupid enough to voice her opinions of him to his face so blithely.

'Don't worry about it.'

For the first time Tara saw the harsh features relax and glimpsed behind the austerity the compassion which must have drawn Sue to him. But why had she never told her that he was her stepfather? Did she really need to ask herself that question? Tara thought wryly, remembering Sue's vulnerability.

'Don't wake Sue up now,' James Harvey continued. 'I'm half dead from the flight and all I want right now is a few hours' sleep. Come on.' He paused, hanging back to allow her to precede him through the kitchen door, but as she drew level with him Tara stumbled. His right hand shot out grasping her firmly round the waist. Tara could feel the hard bite of his fingers against the soft flesh of her ribcage, and her heart started to race and jerk, her inarticulate apology lost in the darkness as James Harvey switched off the light, withdrawing the support of his hand. As she turned away his fingertips brushed accidentally against the taut curve of her breast, and Tara shuddered deeply without understanding the violence of her reaction.

He was Sue's stepfather, for heaven's sake, she reminded herself, hating her body's momentary physical response to his accidental touch.

They walked upstairs together, James leaving her on the landing making his way to the suite of rooms occupied by Mrs Harvey when she was at the Manor. It was a long time before Tara fell asleep again.

In the days that followed and she got to know James better Tara gradually discovered that beneath the sensuality and cynicism which had been the two things about him which had struck her most at their first meeting did indeed lie the compassion she had expected from Sue's description. She also learned something about herself, something she would have given much not to learn and something which kept her awake at night and unable to concentrate on her school work during the day; she was terrifyingly attracted to Sue's stepfather. Teenage infatuations and crushes had bypassed Tara completely, so that her feelings for James came as an abrupt and frightening shock; as much for their strength as for their sensuality. She constantly caught herself daydreaming about how it would feel to be held in his arms, to be kissed by his hard male mouth, her body tortured into fierce passion by the expertise of his lovemaking. Such thoughts disturbed and alarmed her, tormenting her to the point where she felt selfconscious and tonguetied in his presence, the disturbed state of her mind betrayed by the swift colouring of her skin whenever they met. Sue, lost in the pleasure of having his sole attention, seemed unaware of her friend's reaction, and Tara alternately longed for and yet dreaded Sue's mother's return.

Sue and James seldom mentioned her, and Tara suspected that the marriage was not a happy one. Why had James married Hilary? Tara often wondered. He was considerably younger than Hilary, an immensely attractive and virile man in his late twenties with a successful business which he had apparently inherited from his uncle. Her mind refused to accept that James might love Hilary. So why had he married her? Tara was not as naïve as her classmates liked to think. For one thing, she was extremely widely read and by no means ignorant of the power that wealth wielded, and yet everything within her revolted against the idea of James marrying Hilary for financial gain. It was none of her business, she reminded herself, firmly closing the door on her doubts, concentrating instead on the heady pleasure of the increasingly precious time she spent with James. That Sue was always there as well did not detract from her enjoyment. Her burgeoning love for James was her own secret and she meant to keep it that way. James treated her much as he treated Sue, although sometimes there was a look in his eyes when they rested on her that made the blood beat faster in her veins, frightening her that he might guess how she felt about him. On those occasions she was more careful than ever not to betray herself.

One afternoon when the two girls had cycled back to Sue's house together after school, Tara found herself alone with James when Sue was taking a transatlantic call from her mother. Tara's own mother was

beginning to complain about the amount of time Tara
was spending with Sue, reminding Tara that she had
important A levels coming up and adding bitingly that
it was a fine thing indeed when a man married a
woman close on ten years his senior and that she had
no need to guess the reason why.

Her mother seemed to have taken an intense dislike
to James. Tara had noticed it on the first occasion that
James had run her home—the morning after his
arrival it had been, and when she saw his lean frame
uncurling itself from the interior of the Porsche car,
Tara's mother's mouth had turned down angrily, her
eyes hard and watchful.

'How's the studying coming along?' James asked
casually reaching for the knot in his tie and loosening
it tiredly. It was June and the whole month had been
unusually warm. Tara's skin had been turned creamy
gold by the sun, a tiny smattering of freckles marching
across the bridge of her nose.

'Fine,' she responded unenthusiastically, absurdly
conscious of the lean column of James's throat where
his unbuttoned shirt revealed the warm flesh. Her
breath seemed to be oddly constricted in her throat,
tiny frissons of awareness shivering over her skin
bringing out tiny goosebumps on her arms.

James frowned, warm brown fingers curling round
her upper arm as he asked frowningly, 'Cold?'

With his fingers circling her skin, the warm male
scent of him tantalising her nostrils, and her eyes on a
level with the darkly curling body hair exposed by the
opening of his shirt, it was as much as Tara could do
to shake her head.

'So what are these?' Tara shivered as James's eyes

rested on the small goosebumps. 'Tara?'

James's hands left her arm to grip her shoulder and Tara knew that he must be able to feel the way her body trembled. Uncertainty and fear mingled in the eyes she kept averted from him, her one fear that he might guess the truth.

'Tara?'

This time there was a husky urgency in the way he said her name that brought new sensations washing over her. She looked up just in time to hear James swear suddenly as he released her, and Sue came rushing into the room.

'It was Ma,' she announced unnecessarily. 'She's sending me a cheque for my birthday.' She pulled a face. 'Big deal—it'll take her all of two minutes to write it out and have her secretary post it.'

'Didn't your mother want to speak to James?' Tara heard herself asking in a shrilly challenging tone that surprised herself as well as Sue.

'Hilary never did have much time for talking to the men in her life,' James responded drawlingly, to Sue's surprised 'No,' the smile he gave Tara mocking as he added, 'Shocked? How young you are, Tara!'

The way he said it wasn't complimentary and there was a closed-up bitterness about his face that warned Tara from pushing the matter further. Sue started to talk about her birthday. She wanted James to take her out for a meal; to take them both out, Tara realised in dismay as the younger girl's excited chatter burst in upon her own private thoughts.

'No, really, she protested. 'There's no need to invite me, Sue . . . I . . .'

'It will be my pleasure to escort you both,' James

interrupted calmly. 'I'll book a table for us. Don't refuse,' he muttered softly to Tara under cover of Sue's eager enthusiasm. 'Can't you see how bitter she feels that her mother can't be bothered? She thinks a lot of you, Tara—and with good reason, don't let her down now.'

Sue's anxious, 'You are coming, aren't you?' only underlined his comment, and Tara heard herself saying weakly, 'Of course I am,' even though she knew in her heart of hearts that she was playing with fire.

Tara's mother, when she told her, made no secret of her disapproval. 'Dinner at a hotel for a fourteen-year-old? Foolish nonsense!' she snorted, and Tara had to plead with her to be allowed to accept the invitation. Her clothes were chosen for her by her mother, and apart from the jeans and tee shirts she favoured out of school hours Tara had very little in her wardrobe other than her school uniform and one or two sensible and staid outfits which she loathed wearing.

Sue, in contrast, had more clothes than she knew what to do with. Her mother gave her a generous allowance—conscience money, Sue called it scoffingly—and when Tara confided her doubts about dining at the prestigious Davenport Arms, which was the town's most expensive hotel, in the childish 'best' clothes which were her mother's choice, Sue dragged her upstairs to her bedroom, flinging open her wardrobe doors to announce, 'Take your pick—there's sure to be something here that will fit you. You're taller than me, I know, but you're so slim ...' She rummaged through the tightly packed cupboard, ignoring Tara's protests.

'Here, try this,' she mumbled, flinging half a dozen

outfits onto the bed and reaching into the depths of the wardrobe to produce a crinkle cotton dress in a cool shade of green, the colour deepening to jade at the hem.

The dress was similar to several Tara had seen in Hillingdon's shop windows—at least at first sight, but when she picked it up from the bed where Sue had flung it, she realised instantly that it was a far more expensive model than anything Hillingdon had ever stocked. The cotton was soft and fine, the full skirt banded with rows of handmade lace dyed to match the fabric, a peasant-style neckline with tiny puffed sleeves was trimmed with satin ribbon, and when she held the dress against her Tara knew instinctively that it might have been made for her. Later she was ashamed of how little persuading she needed to try the dress on. As Sue had suggested, it fitted her perfectly, causing Sue to say blithely, 'There, I told you, and it suits you far more than it ever would me. I'm too plump for such a full-skirted style. There's a flounced petticoat to go with it,' she added before Tara could speak, 'and a toning cotton waistcoat. Here, take them.'

Tara tried to protest, but Sue wouldn't listen. 'If you don't take them they'll never be worn,' she insisted. 'Ma bought them for me—another conscience-easer.'

Tara dressed for Sue's birthday meal without enthusiasm. To her surprise her mother had made no comment about the dress Sue had 'loaned' her. As Sue's birthday had fallen on a Saturday and there was no school Tara had the whole day to get ready. She had never spent so much time getting ready to go out.

She washed her hair, letting it dry naturally, and grimacing a little over its stubborn tendency to curl. Most of the girls at school had short hair, but she preferred to keep hers long. A touch of green eye-shadow emphasised the colour and size of her eyes, mascara darkening her thick lashes. Wriggling into Sue's dress, Tara studied her reflection in the mirror and pulled a wry face. She had forgotten that the style was meant to be worn slightly off the shoulders and the neckline revealed the straps of her bra slightly.

After experimenting for a few minutes Tara was forced to the reluctant conclusion that it would be better to do without her bra altogether rather than risk everyone catching glimpses of her straps. She shuddered to think of James's reaction to such gaucherie; no doubt in the circles in which he moved women thought nothing of a little thing like not wearing a bra. Having removed it, Tara studied her reflection critically. With the waistcoat on she looked perfectly respectable. She refused to think about the softly provocative thrust of her breasts beneath the fine cotton fabric without it.

She had just finished applying a delicate coat of pale lip-gloss when she heard James's Porsche draw up outside.

Sue was seated in the back, but when Tara reached for the door, James emerged from the car and opened the front passenger door.

'Sit in the front with James,' Sue insisted. 'Doesn't she look fantastic?' she demanded of her stepfather. 'That dress really does something for her, doesn't it?'

Tara was glad of the falling dusk to conceal her flushed cheeks. Was it merely her imagination or had

James's eyes lingered deliberately on the taut curve of her breasts?

It was barely ten minutes' drive to the hotel. The car-park was already quite full when they arrived. A uniformed commissionaire unbent enough to smile warmly at them, plainly recognising James.

They were shown to one of the tables set apart from the main body of the restaurant in one of the window alcoves. Beneath them the river flowed smoothly, its banks illuminated with coloured lights. A re-vamped longboat was tied up at the hotel's mooring and there was just sufficient light for them to be able to pick out the intricate designs painted on it.

'What a fantastic life,' Sue said dreamily. 'Always on the move, new faces, new places.'

'What about you, Tara?' James asked. 'Do you yearn for change and excitement?'

'I'd like to see something of the world,' Tara admitted slowly. 'But people are the same the world over; problems don't disappear simply because one changes one's surroundings.'

'Very true—and a very profound statement for a girl your age. What do you know of life's problems?' James scoffed lightly.

The mockery in his tone inflamed Tara's already over-stretched nerves. Perhaps she was being over-sensitive, but it seemed to her that James constantly referred to her age—or lack of it, to be more precise, and always in that same tone of sardonic mockery.

'It isn't always necessary to personally experience something to know about it,' she retorted angrily. 'There's such a thing as imagination . . .'

'Nothing that's worth experiencing can ever be truly

experienced second-hand,' James told her softly, and something in his voice brought the colour surging to Tara's cheeks, forcing her to realise that with James she was way, way out of her depth and that it was folly to treat him as she might a boy of her own age.

To please Sue she joined her in ordering steak Diane, followed by a rich chocolate mousse, although she noticed that James refused the rich sweet in favour of a wedge of Stilton and some water biscuits. In honour of the occasion he had also ordered a bottle of wine—a warm, full-bodied Burgundy of which Sue had only taken a mouthful before pulling a wry face.

James had laughed, and Tara had forced herself to empty her glass even though privately she shared a little of Sue's dislike of the wine.

It was hot in the restaurant and while they were waiting for their coffee Tara surreptitiously removed her waistcoat, conscious that her cheeks were already betraying a heated flush—a combination of the unaccustomed strength of the wine and her own tense state. James was talking to Sue and as she straightened up from slipping her waistcoat on to the back of her chair, Tara found that his glance was focused on her, his eyes probing the soft hollows of her throat and the fragile bones of her shoulders before moving slowly downwards. Her heart seemed to lodge in her throat, her mouth was dry. Under the thin cotton of her dress her skin burned, the totally unexpected burgeoning of her nipples beneath his deliberate scrutiny, flooding her with shamed embarrassment. She longed to reach for the protection of the waistcoat she had just discarded, but her mortification was too great for her to do anything but sit rigidly in her chair, longing for

the evening to be over. Tears seemed to have lodged in
the back of her throat. What on earth must James
think of her? She still couldn't fully understand what
had happened, but even in the midst of her
inexperience she was aware of the sudden melting
sensation in the pit of her stomach, the desire beating
up hotly inside her.

Her hands started to shake, the palms damp her face
paling. It was just a silly schoolgirl crush, she told
herself, something millions of teenage girls experienced—childish really. But there was nothing childish
about the physical longing swamping her; about her
suddenly urgent need to feel James's lean hands on her
body where his eyes had lingered.

'Tara?' She realised that Sue had asked her a
question and forced a shaky smile. 'Are you okay? You
look pale. I was just saying that I'm ready to leave,
unless you want more coffee.'

Shaking her head, Tara fought down the feelings
tearing into her, deliberately hanging back as they left
the restaurant in the hope that Sue would get into the
front of the Porsche with James.

She was out of luck. As James unlocked the car Sue
announced sleepily, 'Mm, I'll sit in the back. I'm
going to stretch out there and I'll probably be asleep
before we get home.'

The night had turned cool, and Tara shivered in her
thin dress as she slid into the Porsche's luxurious seat.

'Cold? The heater will soon be working.'

James made no further comment until he brought
the car to a halt outside Tara's home.

She fumbled with the door handle in her anxiety to
get out of the Porsche, biting back a startled cry as

James leaned across her, his breath fanning her cheek, as he thrust open the door. Tara thanked him without daring to look up, turning quickly to say goodnight to Sue, her slight movement checked by the pressure of James's hand on her arm as he said quietly, 'She's asleep.'

Tara knew she had started to tremble. She started to move away, startled eyes widening as James muttered something under his breath, his arms fastening round her, his lips brushing the slightly parted curve of hers.

His husky, 'I've been wanting to do that ever since I met you,' discomposed her even more. Common sense told her that she ought to move away, to make some mundane comment that would break the spell which seemed to hold them both in thrall, but instinct urged her to remain where she was, savouring the intoxicating proximity of James's body, the heady delight of the hand that curved just below her breast.

'Sue was right.' In the darkness James's eyes gleamed softly. 'That dress does suit you. I like it.' His hand cupped the soft swell of her breast, his thumb stroking lightly over the sudden hardening of her nipple. Tara sucked in her breath in mingled shock and desire. James bent towards her and excitement spiralled crampingly through her.

'God, I must be going crazy! You're still a child . . .'

'No, I'm not.' All at once it was too late to pretend any more, tonight without being aware of it she had crossed the Rubicon that divided adolescence from womanhood, and she knew with an instinct as old as time that what she felt for James was no mere teenage idolatry. 'I love you, James,' she heard herself saying huskily. 'I want you, I . . .'

His groaned, 'You don't know what you're saying,' was lost against her skin as he buried his mouth in the warmth of her throat. Tara knew that she should object, but everything that was feminine in her was glorying in her response to his touch. In the back seat Sue stirred and James drew away. He was breathing hard, a disturbing glitter icing his eyes, and Tara knew beyond any shadow of a doubt that he wanted her.

'Tara, it's no use,' he told her emphatically. 'It just can't be. If you were older, more experienced, or if I were less . . .' She saw him shake his head. 'I just can't do it to you. much as I want you. It wouldn't be fair.'

'So what is fair?' Tara hissed back, for once forgetting the huge gulf between them; fogetting his married status and the difference in their ages and knowing only that he was a man who desired her and whom she in turn loved intensely. 'Is it fair to make me feel like this and then push me away?'

His smile was full of self-mockery. 'Oh, Tara,' he said softly, 'Don't tempt me. It's for your sake that I'm doing this. Have you the slightest idea of the effect you have on me, or just how hard I'm finding it to stop myself from driving home with you and taking you to my bed? I want you in the fullest sense of the word. I'm a man, Tara, not a boy, and I'm way, way beyond playing the games you haven't even started to experiment with yet.'

In the back seat Sue moved restlessly again. Torn with pain and chagrin, Tara pushed away his restraining arm and got hurriedly out of the Porsche, tears stinging her eyes.

In the morning Tara couldn't understand what had come over her. In her narrow single bed she rolled herself up into a small tight ball, groaning with the realisation of her own folly. It had to be the wine; she could think of no other reason for her behaviour. She had actually let James see how she felt about him—no, not simply let him see, but told him.

In the normal course of events she would have spent part of her Sunday with Sue, but feeling completely unable to face James, Tara told her mother after breakfast that she intended to go out for a walk and would be gone for most of the day. Her mother raised no objections; before her friendship with Sue Tara had been a keen walker.

Congratulating herself on removing herself from any further embarrassment, Tara pulled on a casual denim jacket to match her jeans and opened the front door. Sue would think her behaviour odd, she knew, but she could always explain it away somehow later. If only fate would be kind and somehow make it imperative for James to leave the country without her ever having to set eyes on him again!

Tara was so engrossed in her thoughts that at first she didn't notice the scarlet Porsche cruising slowly towards her. As she drew level with it it stopped, and her eyes widened as she recognised it and James. Footsteps faltering, Tara glanced wildly behind her, but it was too late. James was already slamming the car door and advancing purposefully on her, his mouth compressed in a grim line.

'Running away won't solve anything, Tara,' he said curtly, grasping her arm. 'You and I have to talk. I intended waiting until you showed up at the house, but something told me that you might prefer flight to fight.'

'We've nothing to say to one another,' Tara muttered, refusing to lift her head to meet his eyes. 'Please let me go, you're hurting me!'

'I could hurt you one hell of a lot more if we don't talk this thing through now,' James interrupted brusquely, swearing suddenly as he saw her face, and hustling her into the car without ceremony. Tara felt too weak to object.

'Tara.' Through her tears she saw James push one hand wearily through his hair. He was frowning and she longed to smooth away the furrows with her fingertips. 'Tara, there's no need to feel bad about what happened last night, or to feel that you can't face me again. No, don't deny it,' he said softly when she started to protest. 'I've been there—a long time ago, perhaps, by your standards, but I can still remember. There'll be other loves; other men,' he told her softly, 'and you can't know how much I regret . . .'

'My stupid crush on you?' Tara broke in bitterly, reaching for the door handle and turning blindly away from him.

James's fingers reached the lock before her and then curled warmly round her wrist, the pressure of his grip forcing her towards him.

'Tara, what on earth are you trying to do to me—to us?' he muttered savagely. 'You can't be so innocent that you don't know how much I want you; how I'm having to fight against my own desire for your protection.' He grimaced suddenly, his mouth wry. 'How do you think I could live with myself if I allowed what there is between us to reach its natural conclusion? A woman's first sexual experience is something deeply important in her life, yours shouldn't be with a married man who isn't free to . . .'

'Make love to me?' Tara finished for him. 'Don't worry, it won't be. I don't care if I never see you again in my whole life,' she announced dramatically. 'I hate you!'

This time he made no attempt to stop her leaving the car, and Tara walked several miles before she calmed down enough to realise that her childish words stemmed more from pique than any genuine hatred. How could she hate him when she loved him so much? As she tried to untangle her muddled thoughts she knew that James had been right and that there was no future for them; that he was trying to protect her, and probably save himself the embarrassment of her crush on him. And then she remembered the look in his eyes when he had said that she must have known that he desired her, and her pulse quickened betrayingly, a dizzying image of how it would be to have James as her first lover, initiating her into the pleasures of lovemaking, sweeping aside common sense and logic.

It was late afternoon before she returned home, drained and exhausted, but not too tired to dream yearningly of James, crying his name over and over again until the sound of her own voice woke her.

It was lunchtime the following day before Tara saw Sue. The younger girl looked unhappy.

'James has flown back to America,' she announced miserably. 'He had to leave suddenly yesterday.'

Tara's heart plummeted. Had he really had to leave, or had it simply been a fabricated excuse to remove himself from her vicinity? She knew that logically she should be grateful and that he was only behaving as he should, but she felt bitterly hurt that he had gone without saying a word to her.

A month went by, and then two. Tara had expected that her feelings would diminish in the face of James's absence, but to her consternation they seemed to flourish. The mere sound of his name on Sue's lips was enough to set her heart pounding; the glimpse of a tall dark-haired man all that was needed to increase her pulse rate a hundred-fold.

Exams had come and gone, and Tara alternately longed for and yet dreaded the results.

One sultry afternoon in August, bored with her own company, she set out for Sue's house. Sue's mother was due to return at the end of the month. She was spending several weeks in Hillingdon before returning to New York. Would James be with her? Tara daren't ask.

It was too hot for cycling and by the time she reached the house she was exhausted. The sun had disappeared and the air was full of the sullen electricity that presaged a thunderstorm. Tara shivered despite the heat. Thunder was something which had always terrified her.

The storm broke just as she turned into the drive, vivid streaks of lightning splitting the sky accompanied by fierce rolls of thunder so loud and close together that Tara was convinced the storm was almost overhead. She abandoned her bike in her terror and raced for the house at the same time as the heavens opened. On the short sprint to the back door she got soaked, but to her relief the handle turned easily beneath her shaking fingers, although there was no sign of Sue in the kitchen.

Calling her name, Tara waited, trying to block out the sound of the storm. Moisture dripped from her hair and her jeans were soaked at the hem and waistband.

It was ten minutes before she finally admitted that the house was empty. Sue often left the back door unlocked because she had a horror of losing her key and being locked out, and Tara guessed that she had probably cycled into Hillingdon to change her library books or do some shopping.

The sky had turned from brassy gold to dark pewter, the thunder increasing in volume with every passing second. Tara tried to turn on the radio in an effort to distract herself, but there was so much interference she abandoned the idea. A vivid flash of lightning lanced the sky, striking one of the oaks in the park beyond the house. A small terrified scream broke past her trembling lips. There was no way she could find the courage to leave the house while the storm was still in progress, and held rigid with terror, Tara simply stood in the middle of the kitchen, ears and eyes straining to detect some lessening in the fury outside.

She was concentrating so much on the storm that she never heard anything else until the kitchen door jerked inwards suddenly and she swung round at the sound, eyes dilated with fear, her skin stretched tightly over the delicate bones of her face.

James stood there, dressed in a formal business suit, briefcase in one hand. She registered the fact that he looked tired, and then everything else was forgotten as another clap of thunder sounded almost overhead. She screamed and ran instinctively for the protection of his arms, his rough, 'Tara, what the hell . . .' muffled against her hair as his arms tightened round her instinctively, the sudden impetus of her flight rocking him back on his heels.

'Stop it, stop it!' Tara whimpered, covering her ears with her hands to try and blot out the sound of the thunder, terror pouring through her veins like a floodtide.

'Hush! It's all right, nothing to be afraid of,' James soothed. 'Are you here on your own?'

She nodded. 'I came to see Sue, but she was out.' She flinched as another jagged flash of lightning split the sky.

'You're soaked!' James exclaimed. 'I'll get a towel for your hair.' He started to move away, but Tara clung desperately to his shoulders, her eyes begging him not to leave her.

'It's all right,' he soothed. 'Now just wait here and I'll be back in a second.'

He disentangled her fingers from his jacket and walked back into the hall.

A fresh roll of thunder had Tara clenching her teeth and digging her fingernails into the soft skin of her palms. He wouldn't be long, she told herself. What a fool he must think her! She must try not to panic. She was just congratulating herself on succeeding when an almighty clap of thunder seemed to shake the house to the foundations, lightning zig-zagging electrifyingly just outside the window. Tara's control broke, on a terrified scream she flung open the kitchen door and raced up the stairs, her feet taking her automatically to

the room she knew belonged to James. She pushed
open the door without pausing, barely aware of
James's smothered curse or the fact that he was just
emerging from his bathroom with only a towel draped
round his hips, until his hands gripped the soft flesh
of her upper arms as he caught hold of her.

His 'Tara, what am I going to do about you?' was lost as
she flung herself into his arms, shivering with a terror that
obliterated everything else.

As though he sensed that words alone would not be
enough to soothe her, James drew her slowly towards
the window. 'Look,' he said quietly, 'the storm's dying
away. It's passed over us now, we're quite safe, Tara.'

The quiet confidence in his voice reached out to the
wild panic shivering inside her and had a calming
effect. Her terror started to die down and all at once
she became intensely conscious of the hard warmth of
his thighs against her own and the smoothly satin feel
of his skin beneath her fingertips.

'Tara . . .'

She knew from the tone of his voice that in another
minute she would be released and pushed gently
outside his door, and the knowledge was almost
unbearable. She wanted to stay with him; to revel in
the heady pleasure of touching him, of exploring the
sculptured male contours of his body, to feel it
respond to her own.

A tiny inner voice pleaded caution, but she ignored
it.

'Tara . . .'

'Don't send me away, James,' she pleaded huskily.
'Please . . . I've been thinking about . . . about what
you said before you left, and . . .' Head bowed, she

studied the dark criss-cross of hairs curling against his chest, a weak, yielding sensation turning her stomach to jelly.

'And,' James prompted harshly, 'I seem to remember that the last time you saw me you told me you hated me. If you merely want to repeat the sentiment, don't bother, it's one I can easily do without.'

He had changed during the last two months, Tara acknowledged, studying him properly. His face seemed leaner, the bones harder, and there was a smouldering intensity in the way his eyes lingered on her body that she had not seen before.

'I don't hate you, James,' she said steadily, taking a deep breath. 'I love you, and even though . . .' Even though you don't love me, she had been about to say, but somehow she couldn't bring herself to frame the words. 'And . . . I want you to be my first lover. I . . .'

She got no further. Her body was crushed against the bronzed male flesh, James's mouth plundering the soft hollow at the base of her throat, sending flickering tongues of fire licking through her veins.

'You don't know what you're saying,' James muttered hoarsely. 'Nothing's changed . . . nothing at all,' he added thickly. 'I still want you so much it's like a gut pain, even though I know I must be half out of my mind. Stop me, Tara,' he warned huskily, nibbling seductively at her throat. 'Stop me now, for God's sake, because I'm warning you, there's no way I can stop myself.'

'I don't want to stop you,' Tara whispered back breathlessly. 'Make love to me, James.'

The hours that followed were something she had

never forgotten; a time of magic and delight.

James had been a considerate lover, drawing from her untutored body a response that shook her to her soul, drawing her gradually into a melting frenzy of need so that the pain of his possession was quickly swamped by the urgent tide of her own desire. It had been then that he had told her that he loved her; at the same time cursing himself for what had happened. Tara had merely smiled lazily, supine and relaxed, her body still awash with pleasure. For her the regret and remorse had come later—six weeks later to be precise—when she had discovered that she was to have his baby, and she had gone to him to seek his help and advice. But he hadn't been there, and it had been Hilary she had had to face; Hilary who had laughed in her face when she asked uncertainly for James. Hilary who had told her cruelly that she had been merely one of his many brief diversions and that they had laughed about it together; laughed about her.

She had left without telling Hilary the truth. Later from Sue she had learned that James had flown to New York several days before Hilary had been due to leave for Hillingdon. They had met there briefly but not returned together. Tara knew why: Hilary had told her. 'Can't you understand, you silly little girl,' she had said mockingly, 'he's had what he wanted from you—it's over, and this is his way of telling you so. He doesn't want you, my dear; you would bore him silly, all he wanted was a little divertissement—you poor little fool,' she added, 'Did you really think he cared? My dear, if I hadn't been neglecting him so shamefully he would never even have looked at you. Why, it's almost pathetic! What do you, a gauche inexperienced girl, have to offer a man like James; a man who enjoys the best that life has to offer and the women who can provide him with it?'

Tara remembered how she had been sick on the way home, humiliatingly and thoroughly. That had been the night her mother had taxed her with the truth and she had been forced to admit it, and life had never been the same again. She had thought herself grown up the afternoon James made love to her, but she hadn't been. She finally grew up in the small living room of her home when her mother told her that she would have to have her illegitimate child adopted and she had refused.

# CHAPTER FIVE

THE sound of footsteps approaching her bedroom door alerted Tara to the fact that she was no longer alone. Dragging her thoughts away from the past, she shivered slightly as she opened the door.

'Feeling better?' Sue questioned sympathetically, adding when she nodded her head, 'You still look dreadfully pale. Your Mandy is a delight,' she added, smiling. 'You should see her with Piers—she's so motherly. Simon's a darling as well.'

'He's very sensitive,' Tara told her. 'Too much so, I sometimes think.'

'At the risk of voicing a cliché, do you think perhaps he needs a father?'

'A man to pattern himself on?' Tara grimaced. 'Despite what the psychologists would have us believe I still think the security of one parent is better than two who quarrel.'

'I couldn't agree more, and I'm glad you're still as romantic as you always were. I'd have been bitterly disappointed if you'd been prosaic enough to say you might marry some pleasant, unexciting man merely to provide the twins with a father. Which reminds me, I came up here to tell you that Mrs Barnes is giving them their tea.'

'I'll go down and collect them,' Tara murmured, following her friend to the door.

'Tara——' She paused, turning to glance at Sue's

faintly clouded face. 'Do you find James much changed?' Sue asked her hesitantly. 'Alec says I'm imagining things, but there seems to be something different about him.'

'It's so long since I last saw him that I'm bound to find him changed,' Tara told her in a clipped voice.

'He never married again after Mother, you know, and yet I distinctly remember overhearing Mother tell him in the middle of a row that she'd never divorce him to let him go and marry someone else, so he must have thought about it.'

'And changed his mind when he realised what he was giving up,' Tara suggested sardonically, immediately wishing the words unsaid when Sue stared at her reproachfully.

'Tara!' There was shock and disbelief in her voice. 'I know some people thought that James married Mother for her money, but I never expected you'd be one of them. You always seemed to get on so well. You know,' she added thoughtfully, 'I always had the impression that there was some mystery about their marriage. One moment Mother had gone to the States on business—something to do with the death of one of her partners—and the next she was back, married to James, and yet I can never remember them actually seeming happy together.'

It was natural that Sue should want to make excuses for James, Tara thought tiredly—hadn't she once done exactly the same? His marriage had been the one thing they had never talked about. The young possessed a wonderful facility for seeing only what they wanted to see, she thought cynically, but James hadn't been a young teenager; how had he managed to blinker himself to the reality of his marriage? Or hadn't it been necessary? Why fool herself, she had never been anything more than a simple entertaining interlude, a momentary diversion, the piquant sensation of being the subject of a young girl's love.

'Oh, I know James and Mother couldn't have married for love,' Sue was saying, 'but I can't believe that he married her purely for financial gain.'

'No indeed,' Tara agreed blandly. 'I doubt that purity had much to do with his motives at all!'

Sue pulled a face as she opened the kitchen door. All three children were seated round a large well scrubbed table. The kitchen was decorated in an attractive farmhouse style, and Mrs Barnes, the housekeeper, smiled warmly as Sue and Tara walked in.

'Mummy, I've eaten all my tea,' Mandy announced importantly, 'and helped to feed Piers. Simon has been playing . . .'

'No, I haven't,' Simon interrupted, scowling horribly at his sister.

'Then why haven't you eaten that?' Mandy demanded triumphantly, pointing to several small pieces of carrot still on Simon's plate.

'Because I'm not hungry,' Simon countered, while Tara hid a sympathetic smile. Simon wasn't over-fond of carrots, and she was forced to hide another smile when Mandy announced, 'Simon can't have any icecream if he doesn't eat his carrots, can he, Mummy?'

She had just finished pointing out that since Mandy herself had been allowed a bar of chocolate earlier in the week even though she hadn't been able to eat her sprouts, it was hardly fair to demand now that Simon be deprived of his treat simply because he disliked carrots, when Alec and James came into the kitchen, the dog at their heels. The labrador made straight for Simon, tongue lolling as she sat expectantly at his side, eyeing the despised carrots with a hopeful gleam in sherry brown eyes.

Alec pounced on his son, drawing shrill screams of pleasure from the little boy as his father hoisted him on to his shoulder.

'Alec you'll make him sick, he's only just finished eating,' Sue protested. 'Put him down.'

Simon was engrossed in the dog, Sue and Alec in their son. At the opposite end of the table, Mandy, sturdy independent Mandy, glanced from her high stool down to the floor and then hopefully, enchantingly up at James's lean height. Tara felt a huge lump come into her throat, and something raw and painful turned over in her breast.

'Mandy——' she began warningly, but it was already too late. Mandy had turned to James, a winsome smile planting dimples either side of her upturned mouth, her arms stretching upwards imperiously.

Tara's heart quaked for her small, so vulnerable daughter. Never in all her six years had Mandy ever made the slightest gesture of appeal to a member of the despised male sex, and Tara wished with all her heart that she had not chosen to make her first to James Harvey of all people.

She saw James step forward and then grimace, his eyes hooded and unreadable as he turned away from the small girl.

Mandy's face dropped, tears filling her eyes and, her maternal instincts up in arms, Tara rushed forward, clasping Mandy in her arms and swinging her down to the floor, her expression bitter with indignation and contempt as her eyes clashed hotly with James's.

Later when they were getting the children ready for bed, Sue, who had obviously witnessed the incident, said uncertainly, 'I can't understand what's come over James. He's always seemed so fond of children.'

'As long as they're not mine,' Tara supplied acidly.

'I just don't understand it,' Sue repeated. 'It's so out of character.'

Not as far as she was concerned, Tara reflected grimly. Unlike Sue she was under no delusions as to James's true character. Behind that handsome face, that virilely male body lay nothing but an arid desert incapable of supporting any real emotion.

She dressed for dinner reluctantly. At best it could only be an awkward meal. Sue was already aware of the emnity which existed between her two guests; and Tara could not forgive James for the way he had deliberately turned his back on Mandy—on his own child. She tugged impatiently at her hair, anger sparkling in the jade depths of her eyes as she applied eye-shadow and mascara.

Sue had said that while they invariably changed for dinner when they were in the country it was only into clothes they could relax in, and with this in mind Tara elected to wear a dress which had been one of the 'free samples' she had been given by one of the fashion houses. Designed along the lines of an Eastern kimono, the heavy cream silk was embroidered delicately with flowers and butterflies in soft iridescent colours that caught the light whenever Tara moved.

The gown was tied with a matching sash and secured by hidden press-studs. Tara had worn it on several occasions and felt extremely comfortable in it. Fastening her hair into a smooth chignon, she checked her appearance again in the mirror before stroking her throat and wrists with Van Cleef's 'First', a Christmas present from Chas, and then feeling that she had done all she could to prepare herself for the evening ahead, Tara slipped on a pair of high-heeled gold sandals and opened her bedroom door. Her heart dropped as she saw James on the point of leaving his room. A narrow-fitting velvet jacket and narrow tapering dark trousers added to his height, emphasising the subtle play of muscles beneath the tailored fabric. He paused as he saw Tara approach, his eyes moving slowly over her body.

Tara felt as though she were frozen to the spot, completely incapable of moving, forced to suffer the hated subjugation to his will as his glance stroked mercilessly over every inch of her body, leaving her nerve endings acutely sensitised to the aura of raw maleness emanating from him. An electric silence seemed to spread out around them, even the sound of her own heartbeat unnaturally loud in her ears.

Somewhere in the distance Tara registered the opening of a door, and then Sue's voice shattered the silence, her generous,

'Tara, you look fantastic—where did you get that gorgeous creation from?' restoring some semblance of normality to the atmosphere. Drawing a shuddering breath, Tara managed to find the coherency to explain how she had come by her gown.

'A perk?' James sneered openly. 'And that satisfies you? Being paid for your services with a handful of cast-off dresses? My dear, you've sold yourself cheap indeed.'

'James!' Sue looked shocked and upset. 'Tara, I'm . . .'

'Forget it,' Tara told her, forcing a smile. 'Contrary to what James seems to suppose, Chas pays me for my work,' she emphasised the word deliberately, 'in the usual coinage—and neither am I his mistress, paid or otherwise. Even if I wanted to have an affair with Chas, I wouldn't,' she added for good measure. 'I've got the twins to think about, and I happen to think that children learn best by example.'

'Very noble,' James sneered. 'Quite a metamorphosis. When did it come about?'

'James . . .'

There was no mercy in the look he turned upon Tara, when Sue murmured his name James's expression softened, his arm coming round her shoulders in an affectionate gesture that filled Tara with a welter of conflicting emotions.

'Don't look so worried,' he told her. 'Tara's tougher than you think. Aren't you?'

There was no kindness in the dark blue eyes as they held her captive and to her horror Tara felt tears burning the back of her throat.

She managed to make some brittle comment, something cynical and mocking which brought an uncertain smile to Sue's lips, and as though that exchange had set the tone for the evening it passed in a state of armed guardedness which made Tara's skin prickle with tension. And to think she had come away this weekend to try and relax! She was beginning to think she might have been better off with Chas after all. Her expression must have betrayed her, because Alec teased suddenly, 'Where did you go—you looked almost wistful?'

'I was thinking of Chas,' Tara said without thinking. 'I was supposed to spend the weekend with him.' She was about to add that they had been going to work when she saw James's cynical grimace, contempt darkening his eyes as he murmured for her ears alone, 'What was that you were saying before dinner? It's always advisable when you tell lies to at least remember some of them.'

'Thanks,' Tara replied sweetly in the same low voice. 'I take it you're speaking with the benefit of experience.'

It was worse, far worse than she had imagined it could be, she acknowledged shakily when they were all sitting in the drawing room. Alec had insisted on pouring her a large brandy, and that, on top of the wine they had had with the meal, had combined to make her feel distinctly lightheaded. Tomorrow the first thing she was going to do was to make some excuse for returning home. There was simply no way she could endure another twenty-four hours in James's company. How dare he look at her with such contempt and loathing, such derision, when she was the one with the grievance, with the right to feel those emotions? Tara drank her brandy slowly. The rich warm liquid fired the anger burning up inside her. Quite when anger turned to drowsiness she didn't know. One moment she had been listening in a desultory fashion to the conversation between Alec and James. Alec, it was apparent, held James in high regard—Sue had gone to see Mrs Barnes about the arrangements for breakfast—and the next waves of drowsiness were sweeping over her, drowning out the low hum of male voices until consciousness faded.

In some dim and distant fashion Tara was aware of being lifted and carried, of a warm comforting sound against her ear, like the echo of a sea-shell found on the beach. For the first time in years she felt warm and safe. She murmured something in her sleep, curling inwards to the source of the warmth, muttering protestingly as the warmth was removed.

'Tara.' The coolly firm male voice was familiar and not to be ignored. Reluctantly she opened her eyes, shock widening them and darkening the pupils to jade as she realised that she was lying fully dressed on her bed with James leaning over her.

'Relax,' he told her sardonically as she tensed and edged away. 'You're quite safe.' The cynical look in his eyes brought a vivid flush of colour to her pale cheeks. 'Or perhaps that's it,' James said softly, studying her rich colour with hard eyes. 'Perhaps you don't want to be safe, eh, Tara?'

'Get out of my room.' Even to her own ears her voice sounded shaky rather than firm. 'Just get out,' she reiterated huskily.

When he had gone she lay staring at the ceiling, forcing herself not to remember how it had felt to be held in his arms, but the moment she closed her eyes it swept over her in shuddering waves; the sensation of being held close to him, of being safe. With a tortured groan Tara rolled over, trying to blot out the memories.

'After we've had breakfast, I'm going to take Misty for a walk by the lake,' Simon announced proudly over his cornflakes. Tara smiled at him, mentally wondering just what sort of pressure she was going to be subjected to once they got home concerning the addition of a puppy to their household.

'Oh, that reminds me, James,' Sue murmured, 'There was a phone call for you this morning.' She pulled a slight face as she turned to Tara, 'A neighbour of ours, who seems to have attached herself to James.'

'Yes, I believe we met her yesterday,' Tara responded, allowing herself a tight smile. 'They make a very . . . well matched couple.'

She could tell that James was looking at her, but she refused to return it. Much to her amazement Mandy, despite James's rejection of her the previous evening, was doing her level best to engage his attention.

Tara watched them out of the corner of her eye, burningly resentful when James tried to ignore Mandy's beguiling smiles. Was it because Mandy was her daughter? she wondered bitterly. Poor little Mandy, she had no idea of her handicap.

'I'm going for a walk after breakfast,' Mandy announced to James. 'Do you like going for walks?'

'Mr Harvey is far too busy to go for walks with little girls,' Tara interrupted hastily, trying to divert Mandy's attention, but the little girl clung to the subject like a limpet.

'Why not?' she demanded with enquiring eyes. 'Doesn't he like little girls?'

'She certainly knows how to load her questions, doesn't she?' Sue murmured under her breath to Tara. 'And will you look at James? Game, set and match to Mandy in one go, I believe!'

A sudden wail from Piers saved James from having to reply, and watching him hold the little boy as Sue retrieved the toy her son had flung to the floor, Tara felt a sharp pain stabbing through her. While his own children were ignored and unwanted James lavished time and affection on Susan's little boy. Telling herself that she was being ridiculous, Tara got up abruptly. She was glad James would be going out, that would make it much easier for her to make her excuses to Sue and leave early. She could pack their things while the twins went for their walk.

'Don't worry about them, they'll be quite safe in the garden,' Sue assured her.

From her window Tara had an excellent view of the garden and the attractive lily-strewn pool. Guessing that Sue would be busy with her son for some time after breakfast, she decided to wait for half an hour or so before broaching the subject of their departure. She was packing the twins' case when something drew her to the window. Glancing out of it, she studied the countryside. One could forget how fresh and green everything was, living in London. If her dream ever came true and she was able to set up her own business it would be somewhere quiet; some small market town where Simon could have a dog and . . . A dog! Her heart suddenly thudded heavily as she saw Misty rushing excitedly into the pool after an inaccurately thrown stick. The dog was paddling vigorously, its golden tail sweeping the still water. A terrible sense of dread suddenly swept over Tara, and her blood turned to ice as some sixth sense kept her glued to the window, sick terror rising up inside her as she saw Mandy's familiar dungaree-clad frame wading purposefully after the dog. She opened her window and called, but it was obvious that the little girl couldn't hear her.

Filled with sick panic, Tara flung open her door and ran swiftly downstairs. The dog had been swimming, not paddling, and Mandy wasn't much taller than the labrador.

Thoughts, wild and terrible, flashed through her mind in the precious minutes it took her to race down the path towards the lake, her heart pounding like a drum, the same refrain falling over and over again from tense lips, 'Please God, don't let any harm come to her, please, please God!'

Sue and Alec, alerted by her frantic race through the house, were somewhere behind her, but when Tara reached the pool there was no sign of the blue dungarees or the dark-haired little girl. Fear clawed at her, icy terror flooding through her veins.

'Mum, over here!' She responded automatically to Simon's high-pitched cry, turning towards the sound.

Some bushes shielded him from her view. She pushed past them, careless of scratches on her arms and legs. Simon was standing on the grass behind the bushes. Lying at his side was a wet and obviously chastened Misty and several yards away lay a tiny limp figure like a boneless rag doll, a tall man on his haunches beside her, jeans plastered wetly to his legs as he bent over her tiny figure.

'Mandy!'

The cry was torn from her lips, as Sue and Alec reached her, Sue's arm going protectively round her shoulders.

'James?'

There was an urgent question in Alec's voice as he hurried across the grass.

'She's all right,' James assured them without turning. 'Just shocked and frightened. She didn't realise the water was so deep. She saw Misty go in . . .'

Tara shuddered and broke free of Sue to go and kneel beside Mandy's prone form. 'I know,' she said huskily. 'I saw it all from my window; I guessed what was going to happen, but there wasn't a thing I could do . . .'

'Mandy wanted to get Misty's stick,' Simon interpolated in an uncertain voice. 'It was floating away.'

How many times had she warned them against the dangers of water? Tara wondered tiredly, but it was no use blaming the twins. The blame was hers. If anything had happened to Mandy! She shuddered deeply. If she hadn't been so wrapped up in her own thoughts, so selfishly determined to put as much distance between James and herself as she could . . . Mandy stirred and opened her eyes.

'Mandy!' Tears rose in Tara's eyes, as her self-control threatened to give way. 'I'll take her upstairs,' she began, but it was James who lifted the slight body in his arms, his eyes unexpectedly tender, before he veiled his expression from her with lashes which she had always maintained were far too thick and long for any man.

'There's no need——' she began formally, but

Mandy herself overruled her by murmuring huskily, 'No, Mummy, I want James to carry me.'

Upstairs in the twins' bedroom James placed Mandy carefully on the bed.

'I'll get Doctor Lewis out just to take a look at her,' Sue announced.

The blue dungarees were filthy and soaking, and Tara stripped them off, running a bath in the adjacent bathroom. A subdued and worried Simon had crept into the room and was sitting down watching Mandy's pale face.

James turned to go, but Mandy started to protest so much that he turned back.

'I want James to give me my bath,' Mandy announced. There was a hectic flush on her cheeks, and fresh alarm flared as Tara saw it.

'James has got to go out,' Tara reminded her. 'And you haven't thanked him yet for rescuing you. I still don't understand how you managed to get there before me,' she told him. 'I was watching from my bedroom.'

'So was I,' James told her grimly, 'but I used the backstairs—much quicker. It's all right,' he told her when Mandy made another plea for his company, 'I'm not going out, as it happens. Come on, young lady!' He scooped Mandy up in his arms and, watching him, Tara could almost have believed she had imagined the dislike with which he had looked at the little girl only the previous day.

When Doctor Lewis arrived he pronounced Mandy to be suffering from nothing more than too much pond water and mild shock. 'Kids are blessedly resilient,' he told Tara sympathetically, eyeing her pale cheeks. 'Far less vulnerable than we tend to think, although they can tend to play up a bit. I dare say they'll give you more than the odd grey hair before they're done,' he added to James with a grin.

Shock wrenched through Tara, her eyes widening and fastening on James's as he frowned slightly. With every thud of her heart she expected the doctor to comment on the likeness between James and Simon, so absurdly his father in miniature that Tara couldn't believe James himself couldn't see it, but to her relief he said nothing. Although when Sue had escorted the doctor back downstairs, Simon frowned consideringly and said questioningly, 'Why did the doctor think James was our daddy? Doesn't he know we haven't got one?'

'I don't think he does, darling.' Tara bent down, ruffling the dark hair, keeping her face deliberately averted from James.

'I wish we did have a daddy,' Simon sighed wistfully. 'If we had a daddy we could live in the country and have a dog.'

'I can't honestly see Chas Saunders providing either of those requirements,' James murmured dulcetly in Tara's ear as he turned to leave the room. 'Can you?'

The warmth of his breath against her ear caused her to shiver faintly. Now that the ordeal was over and Mandy was safe reaction had set in. Her legs felt like jelly, the cessation of adrenalin being pumped into her veins inducing a lethargic and shivery sensation that made her long to lie down on her own bed.

The atmosphere during lunch was slightly subdued. At least she need not fear that Sue would repeat her invitation, Tara thought inwardly, toying with the delicious seafood salad Mrs Barnes had prepared without the enthusiasm the food warranted.

'When I think what might have happened!' Sue commented, shuddering as she voiced all their thoughts. 'I won't be able to rest until that pool is filled in, Alec.'

'You need eyes in the back of your head with kids about,' Alec agreed, bending to grin at Simon. 'Kids and dogs, who'd have them?'

For Simon's sake Tara was trying to behave as normally as she could.

After lunch she excused herself to slip upstairs and check on Mandy, who was still sleeping, and when she returned, to her surprise she heard Simon's voice coming from the library, the high-pitched boyish tones mingling with the deeper, more measured timbre of James's.

'James is teaching me to play chess,' Simon announced importantly when Tara put her head round the door.

'And he's proving an extremely adept pupil,' James informed her, the smile he gave his son for a few brief seconds transporting her to the past to the James she had once known, although the smile was doused when he turned to her.

'Did my daddy like chess?' Simon asked her curiously.

Tara swallowed hard, dragging her eyes away from James's lean fingers toying with one of the small black pawns, her whispered 'Yes', a brief whisper of sound. Dear God, she had thought she had known pain, but it had been nothing to this raw agony she was experiencing now. What was the matter with her? Was she still stupid enough to believe in fairy godmothers who had only to wave their magic wands and everything was rosy? What did she want? It was a question she daren't answer, and one that haunted her all through the long afternoon.

It was a relief to go to bed and know that in the morning she would be returning to London with the weekend safely behind her. Apart from the trauma of Mandy's accident it had raised too many ghosts, brought too much fresh pain. With sudden terrible clarity she remembered those first few seconds when she had seen Mandy lying on the grass; when James had moved towards her, grasping her arms, his grip somehow comforting and reassuring; her body turning traitor as it responded instinctively to the lean masculinity of the hands gripping her arms.

# CHAPTER SIX

SOME time during the early hours Mandy's thin, high-pitched cry brought her from sleep, her reactions automatic as she hurried towards the twins' room.

The bedroom door was already open when she reached it, but that fact didn't register until she was inside and saw the tall male figure bending over the narrow single bed.

'Mummy!' Silently, Tara took the precious weight of her daughter from James, rocking her much as she had done when she was a baby. Mandy's crying had woken Simon, who was sitting up in bed, rubbing sleepily at his eyes.

It took half an hour to settle Mandy back in bed and asleep. James had slipped away quietly while Tara was talking to Mandy, soothing and comforting her.

'It was all dark and wet, Mummy,' Mandy told her, shivering, 'and I thought I was never going to escape . . .'

Making sure that both twins were asleep, Tara switched off the light and hurried back to her own room. Once there she couldn't sleep. A warm bath would help to relax her, she decided, but later, sheathed in her silk negligee set, droplets of water gleaming on her skin, Tara acknowledged that she was no nearer sleep, her nerves were still tense. There was a brief tap on her bedroom door and as she swung round it opened to admit James, a beaker in one hand.

'A malted drink,' he informed her, proffering the beaker. 'I heard you moving about and guessed you were having trouble getting to sleep. It must be hard for you, trying to bring up the twins on your own.' The terse admission touched the inner core of pain she tried so hard always to deny, her fingers trembling as she took the beaker and thanked him coolly.

'Look——' He raked angry fingers through his hair, his expression bitter and compressed. 'We're both adults now, Tara,' he said grittily, 'we both inhabit the same league—for God's sake can't we at least make an effort to treat one another as normal human beings?'

His words caught her off guard. She turned, to hide her expression from him, and stumbled awkwardly against him, her foot catching in the hem of the skirt. He reached instinctively to catch her, steadying her, mockery lightening his eyes as he drawled softly, eyeing the rapid rise and fall of her breasts, 'Quite takes me back. Remember?' He had removed the beaker from her nerveless fingers and Tara shuddered deeply, wrenching her eyes away from the mesmerising scrutiny of his.

'You might not have changed, James,' she told him thickly, trying to control her shallow breathing, 'but I have.'

'Meaning?'

There was an ominous ring to the word, but Tara refused to heed it. Every instinct she possessed screamed to her to bring this scene of intimacy to an immediate end.

'Meaning I don't want you near me . . . touching

me,' she added huskily, underlining the words by withdrawing from him.

Savage fingers clamped round her arms, the dark blue eyes as cold and hard as steel.

'Oh, you don't, do you?' he murmured softly. 'Well, let's just see how true that statement is, shall we?'

Fear caught her by the throat; a different fear from the one she had experienced this morning, but equally paralysing. She tried to take a step backwards, gasping as her thin cotton robe parted, leaving her exposed to the cynical cruelty of his gaze. Ice blue eyes moved insolently over the soft curves of her breasts, the delicate rise and fall of the fine lace covering them more an enticement than a barrier to the steely probing glance.

Tara reached instinctively for the lapels of her gown, but James's free hand grasped her wrists, forcing them down with a painfully harsh grip, his soft, 'No need for modesty—not where we're concerned, surely?' bringing a sick shudder to her slender frame.

His fingers probed the area already scorched by his eyes, flicking aside the fragile protection of her robe to expose the slender curves of her body in the pale sea green nightgown.

'Silk,' James drawled admiringly, wringing a fresh shudder from Tara as his thumb rubbed sensuously against the fabric covering her breast. 'There are generally only two reasons why women wear expensive nightwear,' he commented sardonically, 'and they are either because it was a gift from some doting male, or because they hope to use it to entice a lover. I wonder which is true in your case, Tara?'

'Neither,' she told him furiously. 'It was given to me by one of Chas's clients and I don't ...' Just in time she caught herself back from admitting that she didn't have a lover to wear the nightgown for; had never had a lover, apart from him.

'You don't what?' James sneered. 'Adorn yourself in silk and satin for the delectation of your lovers? I wouldn't have thought a woman of your experience would make a mistake like that. Haven't any of them ever told you how arousing it can be undressing one's lover?'

'I suppose you're speaking from experience,' Tara grated at him, forcing herself to stand rigid without betraying her body's reaction to its close proximity to his. 'I suppose a man like you would need that kind of deliberate titillation to ...'

'To what?' James mocked. 'Stimulate my flagging desires? Don't bank on it, Tara,' he warned her.

With a tremendous effort Tara managed to summon all her flagging willpower, desperation lacing her voice as she said huskily, 'Look, James, I think this has gone far enough. I'm tired, and ... and I'd like you to leave my room, or ...'

'Or what?' he goaded her. 'You'll scream? I think not.'

He bent his head, the soft words stirring the tendrils of hair curling across her forehead, and Tara froze, her throat locked and aching.

'Well, Tara?'

She stared up at him wildly, still unable to believe what was happening. He was like some dark catalyst, disturbing the even pace of her life, forcing to the surface all the dark, swirling currents she had fought successfully to subdue.

'James, no!' Her hoarse moan only invoked a bitter grimace, the dark blue eyes boring into hers as he paused purposefully, before sliding his hands upwards to grip her shoulders and bending his head to brush his lips tauntingly across the quivering softness of hers while she lay against him, totally incapable of offering the resistance her mind was urging upon her.

'What an excellent actress you are, my dear,' James murmured against her mouth. 'If I didn't know better I'd say you were still that untouched child I . . .'

'Destroyed?' Tara said bitterly, gasping with pain as she tried to draw away, and his fingers dug into her shoulders, wincing as his face darkened, his mouth curving cruelly as he reached for the fragile straps of her nightgown, sneering,

'Very effective, but a waste of time. I know you, Tara, and I happen to possess an excellent memory. How long was it, by the way, before you married the twins' father? They're six, so Sue told me. Scarcely a good augur of your fidelity, I venture to suggest. You couldn't have married him much more than six months after you'd sworn eternal love for me.'

'I never loved you,' Tara lashed out at him, driven by merciless pain to inflict similar wounds to him to those which had just rent her, although logic told her that he was impervious to anything she could possibly say to him. 'I was a foolish child . . .'

'Who turned into a woman in my arms,' James told her smokily. A muscle clenched suddenly in his jaw as he added with a controlled violence that shocked her, 'Did you tell him that he wasn't going to be the first, Tara, and why? Or didn't he care?'

'Should he have done?' Her fear fell from her as

anger beat up hotly inside her. 'Couldn't he have loved me as a person? But then I suppose that's something outside your experience,' she added quietly. 'You aren't capable of feeling that sort of emotion, are you, James?'

The look in his eyes frightened her. She took an involuntary step backwards, which was a mistake as it brought her up against the bed. The smile curling James's mouth possessed a wolfish ferocity that sent fresh fear spiralling through her.

'Perhaps it's time I reminded you exactly what kind of emotion I can feel,' he threatened softly, his hands grasping her waist and then moving slowly up her body until he was cupping her breasts.

Tara hardly dared to breathe. Her heart seemed to be fluttering in her rib cage like a trapped bird. His hands burned through the thin silk, and to her horror she could feel the instinctive swelling of her breasts and knew that James was aware of it as well. His hands left her breasts and as though she were watching a film in slow motion Tara watched him take the fragile neckline of the pale silk and rip it savagely from neck to hem, exposing the pearly outline of her body to his vulpine gaze.

'James!' Her husky protest went ignored as his hands slid over her shoulders and down her back, the hard pressure of his thighs burning against her.

His mouth fastened on hers, depriving her of breath, reinforcing his superior strength. This was not the man she had loved, Tara admitted numbly as her swollen lips were forced apart and cruel fingers captured her breast. She moaned deep in her throat, trapped between the bed and James, every feeble effort she made to escape bringing her into more intimate contact with the arrogantly male contours of his body. Her bruised lips were released, but James did not set her free.

'What's the matter, Tara?' he goaded. 'Afraid that you aren't as indifferent to me as you'd like to think?'

Tara laughed bitterly. 'Aren't I?' she mocked. 'Can't your vanity take the fact that you can't arouse me?'

'No?' Too late Tara realised her mistake. The hands which had held her with bruising ferocity relaxed their grip. 'We'll just see about that, shall we?'

A quiver of alarm shivered through her, but Tara was determined not to give in, forcing herself to ignore the sensual seduction in the way James slid his hands over her body, moulding her to him, bending his head . . .

Compressing her lips, she averted her head, but once again James was too clever for her and the descending mouth touched not on her closed lips but on the sensitive flesh of her neck, moving erotically over the spot where a tiny giveaway pulse had started to hammer rapidly. His mouth moved sensually along her shoulder and Tara felt herself being forced backwards on to the bed. It dipped protestingly beneath their combined weight, sensations she had almost forgotten existed rushing over her as the hard compact male frame covered her nakedness, the brush of the dark hairs covering James's chest and exposed by the opening of his robe acutely sensitising the tender flesh of her breasts and arousing emotions she had sworn never to give way to again.

'Oh no, you don't escape that way,' James muttered

savagely when she turned her head, stiffening her body. His fingers tightened in her hair, jerking her head painfully round and leaving her vulnerable to the possession of his mouth.

She had forgotten it was possible to feel like this, Tara thought dazedly; forgotten how overwhelming and powerful desire could be; how it could sweep aside logic and self-respect and build up into a vortex of need that sucked one down, devouring and possessing. James's weight pinned her to the bed. A faint flush lay across the high cheekbones, and Tara knew with a sense of shock that he was angrily aroused and making no secret of the fact, no allowances for her innocence and youth, as he had done in the past. This time it almost seemed to give him a savage kind of pleasure to let her feel the hard maleness of his thighs and the desire that flamed hotly in his eyes. His hand cupped her breast, his thumb stroking deliberately against the soft pink nipple. Tara bit back a gasp at her body's shaming reaction; at the swelling response of her flesh to his caress.

'You want me, Tara,' he told her thickly, 'and Heaven help me, I want you.'

As his lips brushed tantalisingly over the aroused centre of her breast, shudders swept her, a tidal wave of desire building up inside her, obliterating the intervening years. Suddenly she was seventeen again and desperately in love. In mindless reaction her hands locked behind James's neck, her fingers buried in the thick darkness of his hair, her lips pressing hungry kisses on his skin as she felt his responsive shudder and gloried in the savagely possessive sweep of his hands over her body, willingly yielding up its treasures to his male domination. This time she made no attempt to avoid the heated urgency of his kiss on her body, arching naturally to the thrusting intimacy of his, her hands sliding inside his robe to caress the satin-smooth skin within, reaching for the loosely knotted belt.

Her movements were ruthlessly intercepted, with bruising pressure, contempt lacing James's triumphant smile as he knelt over her, forcing her to submit to his cynical scrutiny, his measured, 'Who can't arouse you, Tara?' drawl bringing a tinge of colour to her otherwise completely pale skin.

What had possessed her? She could scarcely believe what had happened.

'Oh, don't worry, I don't imagine I've performed some miraculous feat,' James told her. 'I've no doubts at all that almost any sexually experienced male could arouse exactly the same reaction.' He released her suddenly, grimacing with distaste. 'I've proved my point—but don't expect me to do the gentlemanly thing and give you the physical satisfaction your amoral little body so obviously desires. I read the papers, Tara,' he added. 'Chas Saunders and his sexual athletics get plenty of newspaper coverage.'

Tara could have denied his allegations, but sickness clung to the back of her throat, a heavy tiredness seeping through her. What did it matter what he thought? she asked herself bitterly. If he wanted to think she was one of Chas's women then let him. She didn't care what he thought about her—but she did, she was forced to admit half an hour after he had gone, leaving her dry-eyed and aching with misery. It was unfair, she thought bitterly. How could her body have betrayed her so easily? How could she have forgotten so quickly the humiliations of the past? The dull pain that nagged at her she tried to dismiss as mere unappeased sexual desire, but intelligence told her otherwise. Her reaction to James couldn't simply be dismissed as merely a physical aberration. Listening to the regular chimes of the grandfather clock in the hall below, Tara was forced to admit the truth. No matter how much she might loathe and despise herself for it, she was still attracted to James, if only on a chemistry-based level which defied logic and intelligence. If mere sexual need had caused her reaction to him she would surely have experienced that need at least briefly during the seven years they had been apart, but she had not done so; not with Chas, not with anyone.

Heavy-eyed and drained, Tara forced herself to chat normally with Sue over breakfast. The younger girl was trying to persuade Tara to make another visit later in the month, but Tara steadfastly refused, pleading pressure of work. Mandy seemed to have recovered completely from her ordeal, although Tara was determined to keep her off school for a couple of days just to make sure. She was flirting outrageously with James, and just for a moment a shaft of jealousy pierced her. Tara was stunned. Jealous of her own daughter—a child? She could hardly believe it, and yet for all James's attention to Mandy, Tara sensed that something inside him was held back. While the twins ate their breakfast Tara took the opportunity to ask Sue in a low voice if she had the number of a taxi firm.

'A taxi?' Sue stared at her. 'But, Tara, what do you need a taxi for? Everything's arranged. James will drive you back to London.'

'There's no need to put him to so much trouble,' Tara demurred, her eyes clashing and locking with his across the width of the table, his smooth, 'It's no trouble, I have to drive to London anyway,' making her clench her hands into small impotent fists. She would have thought he would jump at the opportunity to be rid of them, but for some machiavellian reason of his own he seemed determined to torment her still further.

'Don't you want to go with James?' Simon enquired doubtfully when breakfast was over and she had taken the twins upstairs with her to put on their jackets. He was far too perceptive, she admitted to herself, too aware of adult undercurrents, and she was not sure it was good for him.

'Not want to travel in a Rolls-Royce? Of course I do, silly!' she said bracingly.

This time James made no demur when she slid into the back seat with the twins, and Tara ruthlessly suppressed what almost amounted to a stab of disappointment.

As they drew nearer to London, Mandy started to bombard James with questions, wanting to know where he lived and worked. He answered her patiently and yet his mouth was compressed. Tara could see it in the driving mirror. A hot wave of colour scalded her skin suddenly as she remembered how her mouth had touched it intimately—could it really only have been less than twenty-four hours ago?

Soon the familiarity of the London suburbs began to claim the twins' excited attention. James remembered the street without needing directions and the Rolls came to a smooth halt outside their door.

Without a word he left his seat and came round to open their door, lifting Mandy from Tara's side, the sleeve of his immaculately tailored business suit brushing against her bare arm, sending tiny frissons of awareness racing through her.

She wasn't going to invite him in for a drink, she decided shakily as she slid towards the door. He was placing Mandy on her feet, but the little girl tugged on his sleeve as he released her, lifting her face trustingly as she demanded—and got—a kiss.

At her side Tara felt Simon wriggle impatiently. 'Girls!' he announced scornfully as James's fingers curled warmly round Tara's arm as he helped her out. 'They're soppy!'

'Aren't you going to kiss Mummy?' Mandy demanded of James when they were all standing on the pavement, eyes rounding innocently as she looked from her mother's flushed face to James's set one.

'You're blushing,' Simon accused Tara with mischievious glee. 'Mandy, Mummy's blushing!'

'Stop it, you two,' she commanded firmly. 'Adults don't go round kissing one another—both of you know that perfectly well.'

'Uncle Chas kissed you,' Mandy supplied trenchantly. 'I saw him, when we were supposed to be in bed. I came down for a drink of water and he was kissing you.'

The look James gave her made her writhe in mortification. Tara could remember the incident quite vividly; Chas had come round unexpectedly one evening to discuss the following day's shot—or so he had claimed. They had been sitting together on her shabby settee when he had abruptly taken her in his arms and started to kiss her. She had pushed him away almost immediately, but she had had no idea that Mandy had witnessed that brief, unwanted embrace.

I know it's none of my business,' James said savagely to her in a low undertone, 'but don't you ever think of those kids instead of indulging in your own selfish pleasure, or do you want them to grow up knowing what you are and despising you for it? I'm not their father, but . . .'

Tara started to laugh hysterically. 'That's right,' she told him in a high, almost unnatural voice. 'You aren't their father, and you aren't my keeper!' Before he could retaliate she pushed past him, shepherding the two curious children up the garden path. They hadn't been near enough to catch the fiercely whispered exchange, but they were aware of some of the undercurrents flowing between the two adults. Not their father—no, if only he knew, Tara thought sickly when they were safely inside the house and the Rolls had moved smoothly away. And how dared he take that high moral tone with her when he was the one who had destroyed her innocence—no matter how freely she had given it—and who had then left her to the tender mercies of his wife; a woman who had derided and scorned her until she had stumbled from her presence weeping and humiliated, her pride torn to shreds and all her bright dreams for ever tarnished. And he had known, even encouraged Hilary to behave as she had—that was the thing she could never forgive. Lacking the courage to tell her that their brief affair was over, he had let Hilary do his dirty work for him, hiding behind the pretence of business affairs abroad, letting Hilary rip the bright fabric of her dreams into pitiful shreds. Tara writhed inwardly even now to remember how Hilary's voice dripped venom as she told her how she and James had laughed about her pathetic adoration for him; how James had told her about their affair, deriding her innocence and inexperience.

'Did you honestly think he meant any of it, you little fool?' Hilary had mocked her. 'My dear, James is a man, and like any other he'll take what's offered— especially when it's offered as freely as your body was, but that's all you were to him, my poor child—simply a body; a physical experience. Surely you must have realised that?'

And so Tara had left the house, her plea to James for counsel about the coming baby unspoken. It would have been hard enough to have confided in him believing he loved her, but knowing that she had been no more than a brief diversion; an amusement . . . Her pride had revolted, and even if James had been in England instead of America, and readily accessible, she knew that nothing would have dragged the truth from her.

# CHAPTER SEVEN

FOR some reason Tara found it hard to settle back into her normal routine. Chas, as she had anticipated, was offhand and cutting with her on her first morning back at work, but she had learned to deal with his moods and for all his bouts of bad temper found him far easier to cope with than James. Perhaps because she was not emotionally involved, she admitted inwardly.

The twins too were taxing her patience. Both of them were now back at school, but Simon talked constantly of their weekend in the country while Mandy made constant references to James.

The situation came to a head one evening after they had been back for ten days. Tara had had to cope with a particularly aggravating Chas all day, his mood switching violently from sullen bitter silence to furious hectoring, coupled with an openly sexual harassment which had brought her own temper to boiling point.

Arriving late at school hadn't helped. Over tea Simon was unusually withdrawn and quiet. Watching him push his food uneaten round his plate, Tara forced down her impatience, reminding herself that it wasn't his fault that she had had a bad day.

'Simon, what's wrong?' she asked him at last when Mandy had been excused from the table to go and watch a favourite television programme.

His stubbornly wooden, 'Nothing', accompanied by

evasive eyes and pushed-out bottom lip, weren't convincing, and real concern pierced her.

'Come on,' she said gently. 'It can't be that bad, can it? Have you had a quarrel with Davy?'

Davy was his closest friend at school, an angelic-looking blond youngster with a fearsomely deceptive smile and a highly developed magnetism towards mischief.

Simon's brief, 'No,' wasn't reassuring.

'What is it, then?' she probed.

'Why haven't we got a daddy?'

The unexpectedness of the question had her completely lost for words for a moment. The twins both knew the story of their 'father' and his death, and although he was rarely mentioned Tara had always answered any questions they had raised and had rather prided herself on her handling of the situation and their ready acceptance of it. Suddenly it seemed that she had been congratulating herself too soon.

'Simon, you know why,' she said as calmly as she could. 'Your father was killed in an accident before you were born.'

'So when we were born we didn't have a daddy?' Simon persisted.

Puzzled by his insistence, Tara went carefully over the story she had invented when she first came to London, pregnant and alone. She knew it off by heart and Simon listened impatiently. As soon as she had finished he burst out, 'David Roberts says that children who don't have fathers when they're born are bastards.'

It was obvious that while Simon was unaware of the true meaning of the word he had just quoted, he knew that it conveyed some insult, and worse, set him apart from his peers.

Tara was at a loss to handle the situation. On more than one occasion she had lain sleepless at night wrestling with her conscience and with the fairness of withholding from the twins the circumstances of their birth, especially as they grew older. She knew instinctively that they would want to seek a closer identity with their father when they were older—she would have done herself—but she had told herself that by lying to them she was saving them the inevitable heartbreak of being rejected by James, and the events of the weekend had only reinforced that decision. James had made it more than plain that he wished to remain aloof from them—and his attitude had hurt, which was ridiculous really—after all, he had no idea that they were his children. But even had he done so Tara could not envisage him acting any differently, there had been more than mere indifference in his behaviour, and she suspected his attitude sprang from the fact that they were her children.

Trying to sound as calm as possible, she gently reassured Simon, taking care to stress the fact that David Roberts had been wrong, without placing too much importance on the slur of illegitimacy.

'Well, if we did have a daddy, why don't we have any photographs of him?' Mandy asked, having wandered in from the other room, and fixing her mother with accusing eyes so like her father's that for a moment Tara felt almost flustered.

Her story had always been that hers had been a whirlwind courtship and marriage with her husband departing overseas almost immediately after the honeymoon, and so she was able to say quickly, 'There just wasn't time.' Her mythical husband had supposedly been an orphan, a move which Tara had felt would satisfactorily explain away the lack of paternal family as the children grew, but coupled with the twins' grudging acceptance of her story was guilt because she was lying to them, and not for the first time she questioned the wisdom of her decision to conceal from them the existence of their father.

'I wish we did have a daddy,' Mandy continued, obviously loath to let the subject drop, warming to her theme as she added innocently, driving the breath from Tara's lungs, 'One like Uncle James.'

Tara's heart sank as she approached the school gates and saw Sue talking to the twins. Fond as she was of her friend she was not in the mood for idle conversation. Chas's mood had worsened with the week, and all she could do was say a heartfelt mental, 'Thank goodness it's Friday!'

Sue beamed when she saw her, her smile turning to a worried frown as she saw the tiredness and strain in her eyes.

'Why, Tara,' she exclaimed, 'Aren't you feeling well?'

'I'm fine,' Tara lied. 'Just a little tired. Come on, you two,' she instructed the twins, hoping that Sue would take the hint and not press the subject, 'get in the car.'

'We've been talking to Uncle James,' Mandy announced blithely, unaware of the consternation her words caused her mother. 'He came in his big car . . .'

'And was outrageously flattered by your daughter,' Sue informed Tara with a chuckle. 'It seems he's her number one candidate for a father.'

Fear and pain tightened a stranglehold on her throat, but somehow she managed to force a shaken smile.

'I came a little early because I wanted to ask Mrs Ledbetter if I could take Piers out of school for two weeks next month. We're going to the States to see Mother.' Sue pulled a face. 'A duty visit, I'm afraid—anyway, James was kind enough to drive me down. He'll be here to pick me up shortly ... Ah ...' her face broke into a smile, 'here he is now.'

Tara froze as she turned and saw James advancing on them. He was dressed formally in a dark navy and wine business suit, oddly incongruous among the mothers and children in brightly coloured dungarees, tee-shirts and jeans. Mandy, who had been holding her hand, pulled away and before Tara could stop her she had launched herself on James, who, much to Tara's astonishment, lifted her daughter from the ground and swung her up in his arms. Some sixth sense drew her attention to Simon, unnaturally still at her side, and her heart dropped as she saw the wistful, almost tremulous expression on his face as he watched James with Mandy. As though he too was aware of the little boy's reaction, James put Mandy down and, totally ignoring Tara, and the possible damage to his clothes, dropped to his haunches in front of Simon so that they were on the same level, and asked him how he felt about a visit to the Zoo.

Simon's face was radiant, and Tara had to stifle a swift stab of resentment that James should so easily charm her children.

'You'll have to blame me,' Sue told her, obviously reading the annoyance in her eyes. 'Alec and I have to go shopping before we leave for New York—you know Mother, I daren't appear in anything but the very latest fashion or she'll disown me, and James has very kindly agreed to play nursemaid for an afternoon tomorrow. We'd already decided that his best bet was probably the Zoo. Piers adores the penguins.'

Tara wanted to protest that James should have asked her before including the twins in the outing, but now the damage was done and she could not refuse without disappointing Simon.

'You know why he's doing this, don't you?' said Sue with another chuckle. 'He wants reinforcements.'

For a moment Tara looked blank, and then enlightenment dawned. Sue was intimating that she too was included in the invitation. Anger, and something else she wasn't prepared to acknowledge, sprang to life inside her and speaking without thinking Tara said coolly. 'Then I'm afraid he's going to be disappointed—I've got something else on tomorrow.'

'Then we'll just have to manage on our own, won't we?' said James smoothly, getting to his feet with lithe grace. He towered over her and Tara was forced to tilt back her head to look up at him as he asked, 'What time shall I collect the twins? I thought we'd make an afternoon of it and include tea in the curriculum.'

Tara managed to stammer out a time, too mesmerised by the cobalt depths of his eyes to register anything else. No man had any right to possess such eyes, she thought despairingly; they saw too much, probed too deeply.

The sun suddenly broke through the clouds, dazzling her so much that she swayed. The hard warmth of the arm round her waist, the tangy smell of male aftershave as James steadied her, sent awareness of him rocketing through her, the brush of his jacket against the bare skin of her arm causing her to shiver with a heightened sensitivity that alarmed her.

Sue's sudden spurt of laughter brought her back to earth. 'Do look at Simon!' she urged them. He was studying a small girl on the opposite side of the road, tiny blonde bunches of hair framing a pert little face. 'Children are the most fantastic mimics,' she whispered. 'When he stands like that he's the image of James. He must have picked it up over the weekend.'

An icy shiver turned Tara cold with fear. She couldn't look at James; and she didn't need to look at Simon. She was well aware of how like his father he was.

She must have managed to make an adequate response, because there was no visible reaction from either James or Sue. Calling the children to her, Tara hustled them towards her Mini, Simon still chattering excitedly about the unexpected treat to come. As she unlocked the small car something wholly outside her own control made her turn. Across the few yards that separated them her eyes met James's hard stare. Shaken, Tara dragged her gaze away, trying not to give in to the waves of anxiety sweeping her.

She must be going mad, she decided as she drove home; she must be to think that there had been something even vaguely threatening in James's expression. What possible reason could he have to threaten her? If anything the boot should be on the other foot.

The twins' excitement mounted through the morning to fever pitch, so much so that Tara admitted to a faint feeling of relief when James finally arrived, Piers safely ensconced in the back seat of the Rolls.

She saw him walking up the path through the small front garden; heart thudding heavily against her ribs as she opened the door to him. Dressed in narrow black cord jeans, a matching shirt and a pale lemon blouson jacket in soft, expensive leather he looked years younger and less austere and yet somehow far more lethally sensual. His smile for the twins was warm and genuine, slashing virilely attractive grooves from nose to mouth. A treacherous weakness invaded her stomach as she watched him. What was the matter with her? Surely she wasn't regretting refusing to go with them?

'Ready?'

While the twins clamoured a noisy assent Tara enquired in stilted tones what time she should expect them back.

The look James gave her made her long to hurl something heavy and preferably dangerous at his head. Cynicism burned in the dark blue eyes, disdain etched in the sardonic curl of his mouth. Without a word being spoken he somehow managed to convey the impression that she had some ulterior reason for wanting to know the times of the twins' return. Seething, she tried to control her anger as he told her coolly that it would be early evening before they returned, his mocking, 'Long enough for whatever you might have in mind,' striking sparks of anger in her own eyes.

The twins had been gone half an hour when Tara heard the knock on the door. She had been upstairs cleaning the windows, and groaned at the interruption, suspecting that it was more than likely to be the neighbour who kept an eye on the twins for her and whose husband, she knew, was an avid Saturday armchair sportsman.

Grimacing to herself, she hurried downstairs, flinging open the door, as she apologised for her ancient jeans and tee-shirt, her apologies coming to an abrupt halt as she saw Chas leaning laconically against the door frame, a huge bunch of hothouse roses in one hand and a bottle of champagne in the other.

Her feeble, 'Chas ... what on earth ...' was silenced as he pushed her gently inside, following her in and closing the door behind him.

'Where's the terrible twosome?' he enquired mock seriously, depositing the champagne on the hall table and following Tara through into the sitting room, with the roses.

'Out,' Tara told him vaguely. 'But Chas, what on earth are you doing here and ...'

'Call it a small apology,' he told her wryly. 'I haven't been the easiest person in the world to work with recently, and as one of the models commented to me yesterday, it would serve me right if I lost the best assistant I've ever had.' He smiled ruefully. 'Only a tiny little thing as well—remember her, the kid we were using for the shoe shots?'

Tara did. A tiny elfin brunette with huge brown eyes and a pixie hairstyle whose size three feet were ideally suited for shoe modelling.

'It seems I'm guilty of sexual harassment, among a whole host of other crimes, so I decided to take her advice and come round and offer a small peace-offering.'

Tara laughed, rescuing the roses. 'If this is what you call a small peace-offering, I'd hate to think what a large one would be!' she told him.

'A weekend in Paris at least,' Chas responded with a wicked grin. 'Only somehow I don't think it would have the desired effect.'

Feeling more at ease with him than she had done for some time, Tara laughed again.

'Look, I'm sorry, Tara,' he reiterated. 'I have been giving you a bad time recently, I know. A combination of things if I'm honest—not least of which is your delectably sexy body. Okay, I know it's a sexist remark,' he admitted before she could speak, 'but that's the way I am. You're a very desirable woman, and I found it as frustrating as hell having you working so closely with me and yet knowing that you'd turn a freezing look on me the moment I tried to make a pass. It didn't do a lot for my ego, I can tell you, but I consoled myself with the fact that I probably wasn't the only man you'd given the "touch me not" treatment. Anyway, what I've come round to say is simply that I've come to my senses if you like, and from now it will be strictly business between us— okay?'

Tara smiled at him, wondering with a sudden flash of intuition if a certain dainty, dark-haired model had anything to do with his sudden volte-face, but she was too wise to make any comment, and when Chas suggested they toast their new-found friendship in the champagne he had brought she did not demur, even though drinking Moët-Chandon at three o'clock in the afternoon wasn't one of her normal habits.

It was five before Chas left. They had started to talk about work; and without the sexual innuendo which normally antagonised her so much she had found him such an interesting companion that Tara was barely aware of how much time had passed.

By the time he left she was beginning to feel quite lightheaded—the champagne bottle was two-thirds empty, and a couple of stubs from the thin cigars Chas smoked lay in the ashtray she had had to find for him; the rich smell pervading the room so that Tara was subtly aware of how very rare it was for her to entertain a man even in the most innocent way.

When he had gone she finished cleaning the windows and then decided to have a bath and wash her hair before the twins returned. The arrangement was that Sue would bring them back, so after her bath Tara simply pulled on clean underwear, jeans and a sweat-shirt, leaving her damp hair to dry naturally.

She was just beginning to pick up the threads of a complicated family saga—a book she had received as a Christmas present and which was still unread—when the doorbell rang. Glancing at her watch, Tara frowned. It was barely six o'clock.

She opened the front door expecting to see Sue and the twins outside, but to her dismay only James stood there, still wearing the same clothes she had seen him in earlier in the afternoon, the dark jeans and shirt giving him a faintly dangerous look in the gathering dusk.

Her first thought when she realised he was alone was that some accident had befallen the twins, but before she could voice her fears, James was inside the house, closing the door behind him, assuring her calmly that they were perfectly all right.

'Sue and Alec were delayed, and so instead of eating at the Zoo Sue's taking them to a McDonalds. We tried to ring you, but couldn't get through, and as she was concerned that you might be worried, I volunteered to come round and soothe your maternal fears. It seems I needn't have bothered.' His eyes were resting on Chas's cigar stubs and the almost empty bottle of champagne, and to her annoyance Tara felt herself flush. Cynicism darkened his eyes and she longed to refute the accusations lying heavy but unspoken in the silence between them.

'I'm sure you must have plans of your own for the evening,' Tara managed pointedly.

'Meaning that you have?' James countered softly, crossing the room and picking up the receiver of the telephone, which Tara realised she must have accidentally knocked because it was already partially off the stand, explaining why Sue hadn't been able to get through to her.

'A sensible precaution,' James murmured sardonically. 'Are you expecting the same "friend" who visited you this afternoon to pay a return call, or. . . .'

Tara didn't let him finish.

'For your information,' she burst out angrily, 'my visitor hapened to be my employer. He came round to . . .'

'To drink champagne with you and bring you roses?' said James in a voice icy with venom. 'But of course. Quite natural behaviour in an employer. God, Tara, I'd thought better of you,' he told her, his mouth curling fastidiously. 'I can understand that you want a man in your life—after all, you're a very sensual woman—but Chas Saunders of all people! Have you no pride? Don't you mind sharing his bed with every little model girl who catches his eye?'

'In this house the bed is mine,' Tara pointed·out with syrupy sweetness, controlling her growing fury, 'so the question doesn't really arise.'

'Then perhaps it ought to,' James gritted at her. 'Perhaps it's time you gave him a taste of his own medicine. I can't believe you've become spineless enough to let him flaunt his little affairs in front of you . . . he certainly makes them public enough!'

'Thanks for the concern!' Tara felt a rush of bitter anger. How dared he stand there and lecture her, criticise Chas, when he . . . 'Or is it really as altruistic as it seems?'

The look of murderous anger in his eyes made Tara realise she had gone too far. She stepped backwards, suppressing a small cry of fright as James's hands tightened round the frail bones of her shoulders.

'What are you trying to suggest?' he asked softly. 'That I want to share your bed myself? Why not? It would be an interesting exercise if nothing else—a study in comparisons; the girl you were and the woman you've become. Although I suppose you're going to tell me that if your husband hadn't died you'd never have got involved with a man like Saunders. Strange how women always blame the man!'

Tara tried to respond, but her mouth had gone dry. Tiny beads of perspiration gathered on her skin, fear coiling sickly through her stomach, a fear that was shot through with a peculiar sort of excitement. Nauseous disgust rose up inside her. What was the matter with her? Did she really find the thought of James making love to her arousing? She shivered beneath the crushing grip of his hands, wanting to find the words which would break the spell which seemed to hold her in thrall and yet somehow unable to find them, and then with a tiny inarticulate cry she pulled free of him and ran headlong up the stairs, a petrified creature in flight, unaware of where she was going, only knowing that she must at all costs escape from the menace of her pursuer.

Her bedroom offered frail sanctuary. The champagne glass she had brought upstairs with her and emptied while she was taking her bath—with a ridiculous feeling of depravity—was empty on the bedside table. She stared at it blindly, gasping with shock as she heard the soft footfall behind her and the ominous click of the door. She swung round, eyes widening in outrage. James leaned laconically against the closed door. He had discarded his jacket and his skin gleamed silkily bronze in the vee-necked opening of his shirt. Her eyes slid helplessly from broad shoulders down to a narrow waist and lean hips, stopping short in burning confusion.

'What are you doing up here?' she managed in a husky voice. 'Please go . . .'

'You ran, I followed,' James interrupted smoothly. 'That's the way the game goes, isn't it?' His glance sharpened suddenly and he crossed the room, lifting the glass, his lips curling back from his teeth.

'Very romantic,' he sneered. 'A glass of champagne shared in the aftermath of love—or to give it its proper name—lust!'

'Something you're an expert on!' Tara flung at him, all caution leaving her as her anger welled up inside her, her protests silenced by the swift capture of her arms; the lethal menace in eyes no longer blue but dark, deep pools of rage.

'What are you trying to do, Tara?' James mouthed softly against her ear. 'Provoke me, or arouse me?'

'Neither,' Tara denied, trying to pull away from him, hating the weak, draining sensation spreading through her body; the overwhelming longing to melt against the male form behind her, to be lifted in James's arms and . . .

A deep shudder ran through her, and as though her thoughts were crystal clear to him James turned her slowly in his arms, threading his fingers through the newly washed softness of her hair, his lips a mere breath away as he murmured almost to himself, 'Why not . . . why the hell not?' and then his lips were brushing hers, lightly, almost tentatively, playing on her quivering flesh like an expert on a finely tuned instrument, knowing where and how to draw the most exquisite pleasure from it. Shudder after shudder exhausted her; a mindless, powerful pleasure sweeping over her, her body overturning her will, responding to a mastery it recognised and craved.

Thoughts, half formed and wildly unreasonable, fluttered in her mind like so many moths beating their wings uselessly.

'Tara.'

Her name was a whispered sigh, felt rather than heard, her lips quivering beneath the sensual brush of skin against skin. James's fingers slid from her hair to her throat, stroking sensuously, wild pulses leaping to life in flesh that traitorously rejoiced in his touch.

'Tara, Tara, you're a witch, you bewitch me,' James groaned against her throat, tugging impatiently at her sweat-shirt. 'Seven years . . .' Beneath the fleecy fabric of her shirt his palm shaped her breast, dragging a reluctant groan from her throat.

Somehow her hands were inside his shirt, trembling against the musky warmth of his body, shaping the taut bones of his shoulders, her body trembling as his teeth nibbled erotically at the tender flesh of her neck.

A tinge of colour darkened James's skin. It seemed to burn to Tara's touch. She felt his hand on the waistband of her jeans, and common sense told her she ought to protest, but the hard muscularity of his body against hers, the heated pressure of his thighs, all combined to overrule her innate caution and the sensuous writhing of her body against the tautly male contours covering it brought a jerked protest from James's lips before they were buried against hers, tasting the inner sweetness of her mouth.

Her jeans and shirt fell disregarded to the floor, the hardness of James's hands as he moulded her lissom femininity against the fierce heat of his thighs burning into her like a brand, his dark head bending to the creamy hollow between her breasts.

His muttered, 'Tara,' sent tiny, explosive waves of response shuddering through her, her body pliant in his arms as he dropped on to her bed, taking her with him.

'Tara . . .' His voice was hoarse, forcing apart her closing eyelids, making her focus on the darkly aroused face. 'Undress me,' he commanded huskily. 'Before, you were too shy, too . . . unknowing, so nervous in my arms that I was terrified of hurting you, but now we meet as equals, capable of giving equal pleasure.' His hand reached for the brief laciness of her bra, unclipping it to expose the creamy contours of her breast with their rosy aureole, his quick, sharp breath shivering across her already aroused flesh. When he bent his head to touch his lips to first one hardening nipple and then the other pleasure surged through her in a wave that was almost painful in its intensity; almost too much to endure as he repeated the caresses with growing urgency, his body hardening against her in unashamed arousal.

Lean fingers stroked softly over the gentle swell of her stomach and painful emotion shivered through her.

'Tara, I want you . . . don't make me wait too long,' James muttered against her skin. 'You're a woman now, not a girl, and . . .'

'And that means you can take what you want from me?' Tara demanded bitterly as his words sank in. Anger and remorse filled her. What a fool she had been, to be so easily beguiled by the desires of her own flesh—no, not simply her flesh, she admitted with a sinking heart, but her mind and heart as well. Her reaction to James hadn't changed at all, nor the reason for it. Brought face to face with that knowledge, she was forced to admit to herself why she had rebuffed all the men who had approached her; why she had refused to allow any other man into her life—she still loved James. Loved him and resented him for his callous desertion of her, and now he was back, making it plain that while he despised her, he wasn't immune to her body. She would be a fool if she fell into that trap again.

He felt her body stiffen and raised himself on his elbows, staring into her eyes, desire giving way to biting contempt as he enunciated with icy cynicism, 'So that's the kind of game you like to play, is it? I think I preferred you as you were . . .'

He was up on his feet, his back to her as he tucked his shirt into his jeans, turning swiftly as she reached for her sweat-shirt, disdainful eyes raking the slender vulnerability of her body.

'Why did you encourage me to follow you up here? So that you could turn me down? You needn't have bothered,' he told her insultingly. 'Sooner or later I'd have remembered that taking you means taking something that's been had by who knows how many others before me—and desirable though you are, I've discovered a certain fastidiousness that prevents me from fully enjoying your undoubted charms.'

His lips curled back from his teeth as he watched her, lying stricken like a wounded doe, unable to take in the enormity of his insults. He had reached the door before she recovered her voice, her bitter, 'A very recent fastidiousness, I would venture to suggest—it certainly didn't worry you when you married Sue's mother . . .'

'Why, you . . .'

For a moment Tara thought he was actually going to strike her and cowered back, fear mirrored in her eyes, but with an almost superhuman effort he seemed to gather himself together to thrust out of the room, leaving her alone as she listened to his footsteps descending the stairs, and the harsh slam of the front door, followed within seconds by the soft purr of the Rolls.

# CHAPTER EIGHT

SPRING had given way to summer; in his newly relaxed mood Chas had made no demur when Tara had asked him for time off to be with the twins during the holidays. Today he was in a particularly good mood, she reflected as she heard him whistling in the other studio and wondered now much his benign humour had to do with his growing relationship with Nina, the petite dark-haired model.

He had brought her round to see Tara only the previous weekend, grinning as foolishly as any teenager, and Tara had a strong suspicion that his bachelor days were numbered. At Nina's insistence he had brought the twins a present each; a complicated building kit for Simon and a nurse's outfit for Mandy. As always the twins had been cool towards Chas, although they had both taken Nina to their hearts.

'Doing anything special tonight?' Chas enquired as she went into the studio to tell him that she was on the point of leaving. When she shook her head he muttered something to the effect that he might call round later, although he didn't say why.

Tara had planned to spend some of the summer holiday with her family, but when she reached home there was a letter waiting for her from her aunt telling her that their plans had had to be cancelled owing to the fact that her uncle had suffered a minor heart attack.

A brief phone call to her aunt assured Tara that her uncle's condition was not too serious, but of course it was out of the question to visit him with two boisterous children, and her heart sank as she replaced the receiver.

She was still feeling depressed when Chas arrived, grinning from ear to ear as she let him into the house.

'What's wrong?' he demanded as she made him a cup of tea. 'You look as though you've lost a tenner and found ten pence.'

Briefly Tara explained. 'The children get bored cooped up here all through the long summer holiday, and Simon in particular enjoys staying in the country.'

'Can't you wangle another few days with that friend of yours?' Chas suggested, eyeing her thoughtfully when she shook her head with vehemence. Tara felt sure that Sue would generously welcome a visit from them, but there was no way she wanted to stay with her friend again as long as there was the slightest chance that she might see James. Her face burned as she remembered their last confrontation. And to make matters worse the twins never tired of singing his praises.

'Hmm, well, perhaps this has arrived just in the nick of time,' Chas suggested, handing her a plain thick, white envelope with her name scrawled across the front.

Puzzled, Tara took it from him, putting down her mug of tea as she turned the envelope experimentally in her hands.

'Come on, open it,' Chas demanded impatiently. 'It won't bite!'

Slowly she did as he instructed. Inside the envelope

was a piece of matching notepaper folded in half. A cheque fluttered out as she opened it and fell to the floor.

Totally bemused, Tara bent down and picked it up, her eyes widening as she saw the amount and her own name inscribed on it.

'Before you say a word, it's a bonus you've well and truly earned,' Chas told her firmly. 'Some of those shots you suggested for that last *Vogue* assignment were pure inspiration, and the commissions resulting from it ought to make me feel ashamed that that cheque isn't twice the size it is.'

'Chas . . .' Words formed a tight lump in her throat and she spread her hands despairingly, knowing that tears weren't far away.

'Use it to give the kids and yourself a damn good holiday—you need it,' Chas told her, adding wickedly, 'Believe me, I'll get more than my money's worth back in the long run.'

It was silly to cry, but the cheque and Chas's warmly friendly manner, both so very welcome after the traumas of the last few months, overwhelmed her.

Chas reacted automatically, providing one of the large soft handkerchiefs he invariably had to hand out to the models he reduced to tears, and taking her in his arms.

It was sheer luxury to sob weakly against his shoulder as though he were the brother she had never had, and she was forced to smother a small laugh when he exclaimed in avuncular tones, 'Come on now, no more tears; you should be smiling, not crying.'

'I am,' Tara protested, proving it with a rather wobbly and watery grin.

'Mummy . . .!' Accusing blue eyes stared up at her as Mandy rushed into the kitchen and came to a standstill in front of her mother.

'Why has Uncle Chas got his arms round you?' she demanded critically, eyeing Chas with disfavour.

'Mummy was feeling upset and I was kissing her better,' Chas responded wickedly, deliberately teasing the little girl, raising his eyebrows expressively in Tara's direction when Mandy frowned.

'Something tells me I'm not altogether popular in that quarter,' he murmured under his breath to Tara, when Mandy had retreated. 'And by the way, who's this Uncle James I've been hearing so much about?'

'No one,' Tara lied forcefully, flushing a little as Chas scrutinised her features closely, but to her relief he ventured no comment, simply saying that it was time he left as he was taking Nina out to dinner.

Armed with Chas's very generous cheque, Tara spent her lunch hour the following day arranging for the twins and herself to spend a fortnight on the edge of Dartmoor, a venue which she felt offered equal attractions for both the twins; Simon would enjoy the moor and the wild life and Mandy the coast and the sleepy, quaint villages. She had been fortunate enough to be able to rent a small cottage not far from the coast, and even after allowing for all expenses there was still enough money left to equip the twins and herself fully for their holiday.

Shopping would have to wait for another day, she decided firmly as she glanced at her watch and saw how late it was. To make up the time she had spent shopping Tara decided to work later than normal. A phone call to her neighbour elicited a promise to collect the twins from school and keep an eye on them until her return home. Janice had a key for the house, and Tara had no qualms about leaving the twins in her care.

She was a little surprised by Janice's flustered, almost bemused expression when she knocked on her front door later in the afternoon. Janice was a no-nonsense type, unflappable and possessed of a strong streak of Northern common sense.

'My, my, you have been playing the dark horse, haven't you?' she grinned, rolling her eyes expressively as she led the way into her sitting room. 'And no wonder! Where on earth did you find him?' she added, further puzzling Tara. 'He's gorgeous enough to make me think twice about my Tom—and that takes some doing, I can tell you!'

Tara was just about to tell Janice she had no idea what she was talking about when movements in the garden caught her eye. Her heart dropped, furious anger mingling with disbelief as she saw the twins playing a bastardised game of football with James—a James, moreover, who appeared perfectly at home in Janice's minute back garden wearing jeans and an open-necked shirt, his dark hair ruffled by the breeze and his exertions. As she watched Tara saw Mandy clamouring to be picked up, her face alight with pleasure as James swung her heavenwards in muscular dark arms. How dared he! she thought bitterly; how dared he seek to subvert her children's affections, to alienate them from her by ... By doing what? her conscience demanded sardonically. By playing with them? by behaving like the father he actually was?

It didn't matter; he still had no right, her anguished heart protested—it was wrong, unfair of him to allow the twins to become so fond of him when his appearance in their lives could only be brief. Hadn't she herself experienced the pain of loving him and losing him? Didn't she know from experience how much it could hurt? And yet watching him with the twins Tara admitted that her primary overriding emotion was not fear for the twins, but a gut-wrenching envy, especially of little Mandy, held so protectively in his arms. She was being foolish, she chided herself; how could she be immature enough to be jealous of her own child? Surely she couldn't really want to be in her place. She hated James.

'You still love him,' an inner voice told her, 'more than ever, and that's why you're so jealous.'

She stood blindly, watching the trio outside, trying to assimilate what her heart told her was true. She did still love James, had never stopped loving him, if the truth were known. All those years when she had pretended to hate and despise him she had been merely whistling in the dark, forcing herself to feel the emotions convention demanded of her, but they were unreal, dissolving like the fragile fabrications they were when faced with reality.

A terrible ache began somewhere deep inside her. Janice touched her arm, her face concerned, and she made some light remark which seemed to banish her friend's unease.

Like a sleepwalker she went into the garden, one part of her mind registering with deep pain the defiant expression on Mandy's face, and the worried one on Simon's. With absolute recall she remembered how often she had spoken sharply to the twins whenever James's name was mentioned; how she had stopped them from talking about their visit to the Zoo, and remorse filled her.

Dropping down on one knee, careless of the damp grass and her best suit, she held out her arms to them impulsively.

Simon reached her first, his smile radiant. Mandy held aloof for a couple of seconds, glancing uncertainly at James before running across the lawn to join her twin.

'Quite a touching sight!' James's voice came from somewhere above her, and Tara refused to acknowledge the gibe, although tears stung her eyes. 'What a pity Saunders isn't here to witness it. I hear from the twins that he's an extremely frequent visitor these days; even to the extent of bringing them presents.'

The critical tone of his voice scraped painfully across Tara's already taut nerves.

'What are you trying to imply?' she demanded bitterly, 'That Chas is trying to buy the twins' favour with toys?'

'Hardly,' came the sardonic retort, '*they*'re far too sensible and astute to be open to bribery.'

His meaning was cynically plain and drove the colour from Tara's face.

'Chas doesn't need to resort to bribery,' she enunciated with deadly calm, letting her fury swamp the pain his taunt had caused. 'And I could remind you that you've been very generous to the children yourself!'

This time it was her turn to use innuendo, but her sarcasm was lost on her victim. Grimacing slightly, he eyed her with an icily distant scrutiny before saying softly, 'Unlike your boy-friend, my interest is solely in the children.' His gaze flicked her like a whip as he added cruelly, 'I don't need to resort to bribery to induce a woman to share my bed, and in that regard you're perfectly safe, my dear Tara.'

'As I was the summer I was seventeen?'

The bitter, hurt words were out before she could stop them, and in the ear-shattering silence that followed Tara turned cold with dread.

'You still remember that?'

James's tone was carelessly light. 'You amaze me. I should have thought my image had long ago been supplanted by the man you married so quickly afterwards—the twins' father. What was he like?' he asked unexpectedly, drawling the words in a coolly insulting fashion that suggested that he found it extraordinary that any man should want to marry her. Here was her chance, her opportunity to destroy him as he had once destroyed her by extolling the virtues of her supposed 'husband', but somehow the lies would not come. In her kitchen she saw Janice making a pot of tea, such an ordinary homely task so far removed from her own state of mind and the vulnerability she experienced whenever James was near her.

'Well?'

'Our daddy was killed abroad,' Mandy supplied eagerly. 'Before we were born.'

'And Mummy loved him very much,' Simon piped up, obviously remembering what Tara had told him.

'Did you? He seems a strangely disembodied character to me, far too much so to have generated this all-consuming "love". Did you "love" him?'

She had every intention of saying 'Yes', every intention in the world, but somehow the words would not come, and James was looking at her with sharply narrowed eyes while the world seemed to rock to a standstill and she felt he was looking into her heart and reading the truth engraved on it.

'I . . . I loved the twins' father very much—and still do,' she managed in a husky whisper, only realising when the words were spoken exactly what she had said. Hysterical laughter bubbled up inside her. She had just told James how much she loved him while he, all unknowing, continued to look down the length of his arrogant nose at her, his eyes as chilly as winter skies. How much more sardonic he would look if he knew the truth—that she had been foolish enough to love him then and that she had compounded that folly by loving him now.

He walked with them back to the house, and although every instinct screamed at her not to do so, politeness demanded that Tara ask him in. He wandered into the kitchen while she was preparing the twins' supper, picking idly at the bowl of salad she was preparing, Mandy at his side, saying disapprovingly, 'You shouldn't do that, should he, Mummy?'

'No, he shouldn't,' Tara agreed automatically.

'Perhaps he's hungry,' Mandy added. 'Can he stay for tea?'

'I'm sure Uncle James has other things to do,' Tara told her firmly. 'Now be a good girl and go and wash your hands. We're having strawberries for afters tonight.'

'Really? My favourites,' James admitted, to Mandy's obvious delight.

'Then you are going to stay?' she demanded, all excitement.

James looked enquiringly at Tara. 'If your mummy doesn't mind,' he assented. 'Contrary to her supposition, there's nothing I'd rather do than share supper with my very favourite twins.'

Supper was a hectic meal. Watching James with a twin either side of him in her small dining alcove, Tara couldn't help contrasting their surroundings with those he must normally enjoy. The furniture was old—junk shop bought most of it, lovingly painted and refurbished, but with no pretences to being anything other than what it was. The curtains had been a lucky buy and home-made, she had painted the woodwork and papered the walls herself. She had also sanded the floorboards, stained them and made the multi-coloured rag rug lying on the floor. Up until now she had been perfectly content with her small home and its contents, but suddenly she was bitterly conscious of how shabby it was. Some of Simon's paintings from school were pinned on the wall, a jar of flowers Mandy had picked for her adorning the bookcase. The meal itself was very plain—chicken salad and plenty of wholemeal bread and butter for the twins to fill up on before she gave them the strawberries she had bought as a treat and the icecream she made herself and which she knew they loved.

When it was time to get the sweet she brought in the three previously prepared dishes and a bowl of icecream, placing the dishes in front of James, Simon and Mandy.

'Aren't you having any?' Simon questioned her innocently.

Avoiding James's eyes, Tara shook her head. 'I'm on a diet,' she said lightly. The truth was that the strawberries had been an expensive luxury, barely large enough to stretch to the three of them, and her face flamed as she dwelt on what conclusions James would draw from the incident. There was scant chance of her deceiving him as easily as she had deceived Simon, she thought bitterly, and humiliation welled up inside her as she imagined his disdainful contempt. In the circles in which he moved, people thought nothing of ordering out-of-season strawberries for breakfast if they felt so inclined.

After supper she left him playing on the floor with the twins while she cleared the table. She was elbow-deep in hot sudsy water when he surprised her by strolling into the kitchen, taking up a stance against the fridge, reminding her unbearably of the circumstances of their very first meeting. If she had known then what the outcome of their relationship was to be, if she could turn back the clock, would she? She thought of the happiness the twins had brought her, and knew the answer.

'I'm sorry—about the strawberries.' The husky timbre of his voice shivered across raw nerves, anger snapping in her eyes as she turned towards him.

'So am I,' she agreed evenly. If he thought his comment would embarrass her then she would quickly disabuse him. 'I was looking forward to them.'

Just for a second she thought she saw amusement and admiration, gleaming in his eyes, but it was gone too swiftly for her to be sure she had not imagined it.

His smooth, 'Then perhaps you'll allow me to make reparation,' stung, underlining the huge social gulf between them. She was a single parent struggling to bring up two children on a slender salary; he was a wealthy man, he drove an expensive car, wore expensive clothes. And yet looking at him now, the tanned column of his throat exposed by the open-necked shirt, his folded arms unconsciously drawing attention to muscled forearms, she was conscious not of the differences between them, but the musky scent of his body, the fine tracing of hairs curling over his chest, and the trembling, weakening desire coursing through her to go to him and slide her fingers over his skin into the thick darkness of his hair, to press her lips against the warm column of his throat and feel his body clench in fierce need.

Angry with herself, she tried to stem the feelings growing inside her and said acidly,

'How, by flaunting your wealth? By "buying" me, the way you've bought the twins?'

Scorn trembled through her voice and Tara knew that he was angry. Even so, she was caught off guard when he moved towards her, gripping her waist with fingers that punished her flesh, his grated, 'What do you prefer? Payment in kind?' sending trickles of tension coursing icily down her spine.

She tried to articulate; to demand that he release her, telling herself that this was a ridiculous, farcical situation, but when she raised her soapy hands to fend him off they clung damply to his shirt, his body tautly muscled and warm beneath her fingers, sending erotic messages flashing to her brain until she was drowning in the heady sensation of being close enough to him to breathe in the male scent of him and to be beguiled by memories of the past, rising up to swamp the present.

She must have made some involuntarily movement, some gesture of defeat, because she saw his response to it in the sudden narrowing of his eyes before they dropped to her mouth and his head bent slowly towards her.

She knew that he was going to kiss her, but what she hadn't bargained for was the hard brutality of a kiss that took without giving, ravaging the softness of her lips, reducing her to the mere recipient of some male-driven aggression that found relief in the rape of her mouth. Before she could move his hand stroked upwards, his palm burning into the tender skin of her breast.

Just for a moment she experienced a traitorous urge to yield, to mould her body to his and respond with fierce need to the raw sexuality of his embrace, but just in time self-respect urged her to resist. She was confusing the hard, cynical man who held her in his arms with the tender lover he had been in her youth— and he had been tender, no matter what might have followed later. As though he sensed her withdrawal, James raised his head and stared down at her, studying her swollen mouth and shadowed eyes.

Turning on his heel, he left the kitchen without a word to her, leaving her drained and sick to her soul with self-revulsion because she had so nearly given in to the dangerous undertow of desire whispering falsely in her ear that to be made love to by James once again, no matter through what motivation, was more than worth all the tears and heartache which would inevitably follow.

How could she so easily have forgotten all her hard-earned lessons, have been ready to throw away the self-respect and self-confidence she had built and nourished so painstakingly since the twins' birth?

In the distance she registered his goodbyes to the twins and their disappointed response. It was not Mandy's fault, she told herself tiredly later in the evening when she was bathing the little girl, and she came very close to losing her temper with her when she kept insisting that 'Uncle James' was her very favourite man. It was not Mandy's fault at all. If anything it was hers, but knowing that didn't make bearing her burden of guilt any the easier.

# CHAPTER NINE

FOR two weeks Tara saw and heard nothing of James, and then one afternoon in Knightsbridge, where she had gone searching for some props Chas needed for a 'County' shot he was filming, she saw him coming out of an expensive-looking mews, a slim, dark-haired woman clinging to his arm.

For a moment Tara simply froze, and then realising how easily he could turn his head and see her she panicked, darting into the first shop door she came to.

As it happened, it was a dress shop and she was able to make a pretence of browsing while James and his companion strolled past.

Tara recognised her immediately. It was the woman who had come over to their table in the restaurant the day he had driven them down to Sue's. The dull ache inside her became a sharp pain, jealousy a bitter gall tainting the back of her throat.

When she was sure that they had gone she escaped from the expensive and slightly overpowering environs of the shop. She was grateful for Chas's forbearance when she returned to the studio minus several of the items he had asked for, but one look at her pale face and huge, agonised eyes had warned him against questioning her. He had seen that look on too many women's faces to mistake it, and he found himself wondering about the man who had brought it to Tara's. Outwardly she was so cool and in control;

unflappable and pleasant always and yet retaining a detached, keep-your-distance air that never failed to intrigue him. She was adept at holding people away from her, and yet he had sensed from the very first moment she had come for her interview that beneath the cool surface lurked a woman of deeply felt emotions. Recognising that in her present disturbed state she was not likely to work to optimum proficiency, he suggested they make an early night of it. Surprised, but too wrapped up in her thoughts to question his decision, Tara thanked him.

As though catching her mood from her the twins were particularly awkward during the evening—not just Mandy but Simon as well, and, her temper frayed by her brief sighting of James with his woman friend, Tara snapped crossly at them when they baulked at going to bed. That the battle was a nightly ritual and never normally bothered her was forgotten, their disobedience bringing to a head the churningly disturbing emotions she had been feeling all after-noon—no, not just all afternoon, she admitted to herself as she thankfully closed Mandy's bedroom door behind her, but for several weeks. Ever since she had been forced to admit to herself that she still loved James. Mandy's parting comment hadn't helped either, but a brief smile tugged at Tara's lips nevertheless, as she recalled Mandy's piped and scathing, 'You're just cross because Uncle Chas doesn't come round any longer—well, we don't care. We don't like him, we like Uncle James!'

If only she knew, Tara thought tiredly, regretting her impatience with them. She would make it up to them in the morning, she decided, thank goodness it was Saturday, they could all go out for the day. It would do them good to get away from London. They could drive down to Brighton, play on the beach. It was time she put James firmly behind her, she told herself. He didn't care any more about her now than he had done before—probably less, and it was unfair of her to take her own pain out on the twins.

She said nothing to the twins of her decision to take them out for the day over breakfast, and was glad when she went out to the car and saw with a sinking heart the slow puncture in the front nearside tyre.

Her spare tyre wasn't in the best of conditions, and rather than risk the journey without it, Tara decided to change the wheel and then drive to her local garage where she knew she could get another. She could also fill up on petrol at the same time, and instructing the twins to behave while she was gone, she hurried back out to the car, suppressing a faint smile.

The pair of them had been thoroughly subdued over breakfast, so much so that she had been tempted to plead for their forgiveness, but they would cheer up soon enough when they learned what she had in mind. Her mind on the picnic meal she intended to prepare, Tara completed her business at the garage and drove quickly home.

As she drew up outside the house the first thing she noticed was that the front gate was open, and she frowned. The twins were strictly forbidden to leave the garden when she was not with them. She glanced at her watch. She had been gone just over twenty minutes, hardly long enough for them to get bored enough with their own company to want to flout one of her strictest rules. She must have left the gate open herself in her haste, she reassured herself, but nevertheless her heart pounded sickly and her footsteps sounded anxious as she hurried up the path and pushed open the door.

Silence greeted her, a silence which made her stomach churn in agonised protest, her gaze desperately flying from one object to another as she called the twins' names.

No answer. She hurried into the kitchen on legs suddenly desperately weak. On the floor lay the smashed pieces of a china teapot—part of a set her mother had given her the previous year. The china wasn't particularly to Tara's taste, but knowing how offended her mother would be if she didn't appear to treasure it the twins were strictly forbidden to touch. Her heart lurched into her stomach as she contemplated the broken teapot which she dimly remembered had been wedged awkwardly in one of the bottom cupboards, at a slightly dangerous angle. She remembered that she had made a mental note to move it to a safer place and had then completely forgotten. There was evidence that some washing up had been in progress and it didn't take any great powers of deduction to realise that the teapot had met its unfortunate fate during this operation. Recalling how cross she had been with the twins the previous evening, Tara realised that they had probably gone into hiding somewhere fearing retribution. The thought lifted her stricken spirits, and she hurried upstairs expecting to find the twins in one of the bedrooms, all innocent smiles when taxed with their 'crime.'

The bedrooms were empty, and fear gnawed at her

again. Downstairs she made a thorough search of the house before going into the garden. Could they have gone to see Janice?

Her neighbour was sympathetic but couldn't help.

'The little imps,' she chuckled when Tara had explained what had happened, 'they're probably hiding somewhere in the garden.'

'No,' Tara told her tightly. 'Oh Janice, I'm so frightened! You were my last hope. One hears such dreadful things . . .' She shuddered, burying her face in her hands, making no protest when Janice pushed her down into a chair and disappeared into her kitchen. She could hear her moving about and started to get up, but Janice reappeared, carrying a mug.

'Hot, sweet tea—yes, I know you don't take sugar, but it's the best thing for shock. Look, let's go through the whole thing again. I'll come back with you and we'll go right through the house. Panic makes people do odd things; ten to one they're tucked away somewhere in the house, too scared to come out and admit what they've done. We'll soon find them,' she comforted practically. 'Drink your tea.'

Numbly Tara did as she was told. Deep in her heart of hearts, she wasn't convinced by what Janice had said. The twins had run away, she was sure of it. She remembered how cross she had been with them, how subdued they had appeared this morning and how tragic the broken teapot must have appeared. Oh God, what had she done? Allowing her own children to believe a china teapot mattered more to her than them!

This and other equally morbid thoughts ran through her head as Janice hurried with her back to the house.

Half an hour later Janice, now as pale as Tara was herself, was forced to concede defeat.

'There's nothing else left but to call the police, love,' she said softly. 'Shall I do it, or . . .'

Tara shook her head. 'I'll do it,' she managed in a voice that cracked with pain.

The sergeant on the other end of the line was patient and helpful. 'Just take your time, madam,' he urged her when she broke down in the middle of describing Mandy's pink dungarees. 'I'll send a W.P.C. round to talk to you, but meanwhile we'll get some patrols searching for them. You just sit tight.'

The woman police constable was about Tara's own age, pleasant and yet slightly distant. Tara had to go over every detail of the children's clothing and the events of the morning yet again for her while she wrote it down.

'Do you often leave the twins on their own?' she was asked at one point, and the question drove the blood from her face. What was the woman trying to imply? That the twins were latchkey 'orphans', whose mother didn't care one way or the other?

'Never,' Tara told her huskily. 'I was gone twenty minutes . . . twenty minutes . . .'

Seeing the real agony in her eyes, the policewoman tactfully refrained from pointing out how many other parents had said something similar and had lived to regret those very few minutes.

'Have you any idea what might have happened to them?'

Tara took a deep breath.

'I think they've probably run away,' she said huskily. 'We had words—last night. I was going to take them out for the day today for a treat.' Tears welled in her eyes and overflowed. There were other questions—questions that horrified and appalled her, hinting at child battering and worse, but while one part of her mind was outraged, Tara recognised that such questions were a necessary part of the procedure.

Janice too was questioned. She was in tears now as well, and Tara was asked if there was anyone she wanted with her—a boy-friend perhaps, the policewoman suggested.

Tara shook her head. 'I don't have one,' she told her.

'What about Chas?' Janice suggested. 'You need someone with you.'

Tara explained to the policewoman who Chas was, and as though somehow she were divorced from the proceedings Tara registered the fact that the girl was putting in a radio request for Chas to be contacted, her own voice saying inanely, 'Please don't bother him,' over and over again, echoing in her ears like some vague recording.

The long day wore on. Chas arrived, full of concern and shock, Nina with him. The policewoman disappeared and reappeared a little later, her manner much more warm and comforting, and Tara suspected that she had been doing a little discreet digging in the social service records, making sure that neither Tara nor the twins had any record of past incidents.

'Don't worry,' she was assured over and over again, 'they'll be found.' But would they? London was such a vast place, the twins so terribly vulnerable. All the evils that could befall two young children filled her mind in crashing waves, terror after terror blanking out the sympathy of everyone with her. At one point, unable to stand the inactivity any longer, she begged to be allowed to go out with the patrols, but was gently refused.

'It's better if you stay here,' she was told. 'When we find them the first person they're going to want is you.'

She heard, but didn't accept. She was the last person they wanted, otherwise they would never have run away.

'Their father is dead, is that right?' The police-woman was asking her the question and just for a moment Tara longed to tell the truth and have James at her side to face this terrible ordeal with her, but sanity prevailed and she nodded her head quickly, averting her face, not wanting anyone to guess that she was lying.

'And they've no relatives they could go to who live locally?'

She had answered all these questions already, but sensing that merely the automatic response of replying would occupy and free from pain some tiny part of her brain, Tara slowly responded.

Afternoon dragged into evening. The police left. They would keep her informed, she was told. Chas took Nina home, but then returned, insisting on making a light omelette which Tara couldn't touch.

'There's honestly no need for you to stay with me—I'll be pefectly all right,' she insisted to Chas for the umpteenth time, but he overruled her objections, coming towards her and taking her in his arms.

'For heaven's sake try and let go a little, love,' he said softly. 'This isn't the time to preserve that stiff upper lip act you're so good at. What are friends for, after all?'

She started to cry, and he produced a large handkerchief, pushing the tangled hair out of her eyes. They heard footsteps in the hall, and Chas smiled down at her.

'Sounds like the police are back,' he told her. 'Let's hope they have some good news.'

That he suspected they wouldn't have was apparent to Tara in the way in which he kept his arm round her, holding her against him as though he feared she would break into a thousand fragile pieces.

The door opened and she heard herself repeating the prayer she had been saying all day long. 'Please God, let them be safe. Please, please, God!'

The footsteps stopped and she lifted her head, confusion and disbelief mirrored in her eyes as they met James's contemptuously bitter ones.

'My God!' he whispered savagely. 'Even now with your children missing you haven't a thought in your head but your own physical satisfaction!'

Tara ignored the latter part of his statement, concentrating on his initial words, her croaked, 'How do you know about the twins?' drawing a grim darkening of his eyes, his mouth sour as he told her brutally,

'I know because they've spent all afternoon with my housekeeper, too damned frightened to come home to you, and all over some crazy teapot they broke!'

Anger and pain rushed over her in a massive, turbulent wave. 'All afternoon?' Her voice registered shock and bitterness. 'You mean you've known all afternoon and not let me know? Is this your idea of some sort of punishment for being an unfit mother, do you . . .'

Chas silenced her, his face nearly as white as her own.

'If I weren't a civilised human being I'd throttle you with my bare hands,' he told James slowly. 'Have you any idea of the agony you've caused her, of what she's had to endure today? To say nothing of the fact that half the local police force is out looking for those two kids? You ought to be locked up!' he finished in disgust.

'Uncle Chas, I take it?' James sneered back. 'Comforting the grieving mother. All this performance today has nothing to do with the fact that those two kids don't want you as their father, of course?'

Tara felt Chas's surprise and looked up at him despairingly. He responded with a quick smile and a tiny squeeze of her arm.

'It's what Tara wants that concerns me,' he replied smoothly. 'And I think we'd better telephone the police. You'll have some explaining to do,' he warned James. 'I'm not sure about the law concerning minors, but I would have thought simple common sense would have led you to report the fact that they were with you . . .'

'I'm sure it would,' James agreed quickly, 'if I'd known. I was out of town for the day, and the first I knew of their arrival was when I got home. They refused to tell Mrs Hammond their surname or where they came from—my stepdaughter, who would have known, is away at the moment and she was obliged to wait for my return. When I did return I lost no time in coming straight round.'

'You could have telephoned,' Chas pointed out, reaching for the telephone as he spoke.

'So I could,' James agreed smoothly, 'but the twins seemed rather reluctant to face their mother, so I decided to drive round instead in the hope that I could persuade her to return with me so that we could sort this whole mess out.'

Right at that moment Tara would have promised to go to the ends of the universe with the devil himself if it meant getting the twins back safely.

Refusing Chas's offer to accompany her, she waited impatiently for him to finish reporting the twins' safety to the authorities, so that they could leave.

'They want to speak to you,' he told James, handing him the receiver.

'I'd better go, love,' he told Tara in a low voice. 'Unless you want me to come with you?'

'No, thanks.' Tara smiled up at him, kissing his cheek affectionately unaware of the fact that James was watching him or that his eyes had darkened furiously.

'You just can't leave him alone, can you?' he threw at her when Chas had gone and they were on their way out to his car. 'What's so special about him? Or is it simply that he's good in bed?'

Tara refused to respond to his taunts, huddling as far away from him as she possibly could as he slid into the Rolls.

He drove in silence through the London traffic, and just before they drew up in front of it, Tara recognised the mews block she had seen him emerging from with the dark-haired woman.

Something must have registered on her face, because he grasped her arm as she reached for the door, forcing her round to face him.

'Something wrong?'

Some devil prompted her to say coolly, 'Perhaps I object to my children being exposed to the sort of careless morals you seem to favour.'

She had expected him to let the subject go, but instead he prompted in a dangerously quiet tone, 'I could say I find that remark extraordinary coming from you, but instead I'll ask you to elucidate. Meaning what exactly?'

'Meaning that I saw you leaving this mews yesterday with a woman,' Tara told him proudly, refusing to be quelled by the rage she could sense boiling up inside him but kept tightly battened down.

'She'd called on me to talk to me about some investments she was worried about.' James shrugged broad shoulders. 'An innocent enough meeting, and very far from your fevered imaginings of the two of us making love in my bedroom.'

But not from hers, Tara thought inwardly. She had desired James, and she hadn't bothered to hide that fact from her.

'Any more nasty cracks like that and you'll have me thinking you're jealous,' James taunted as he took her arm and directed her up the four steps to the dark green front door, his threat leaving her speechless with fear.

Inside the house was far less grand than she had anticipated.

Several panelled doors led off the small square hall with its polished parquet flooring and single oval table holding a pot-bellied brass container and an attractive arrangement of flowers.

A flight of stairs led upwards, but it was on the opening door in the hall that Tara concentrated.

Disappointment flooded her as a tall, middle-aged woman walked in.

'The twins' mother, Mrs Hammond,' James introduced her. 'Tara, meet Mrs Hammond, my housekeeper.'

'I'm sorry if the twins have caused you any anxiety or trouble,' Tara began awkwardly, wondering what on earth the housekeeper must think, but her apology was brushed aside by the older woman's rich laugh.

'Well, I was concerned,' she admitted, 'Simply because they wouldn't tell me who they were, and I knew someone must be worrying about them. Too well dressed and polite for it to be anything else,' she added, restoring some of Tara's equanimity. 'But Mandy's a real caution, isn't she? Oh, but you look so pale,' she added to Tara. 'You must have been worried half to death!'

'I was,' Tara agreed, no longer ashamed to admit it, or concerned at what conclusions James might draw from the tears sparkling on her long eyelashes. 'I can't tell you how much, but what I don't understand is how they got here.'

'Apparently Mandy had memorised my address,' James told her quietly. 'They used their pocket money and somehow—who knows how—managed to make their way here.'

Tara's stomach tightened as she thought of the appalling risks they had all unknowingly run, the terrible things that could have happened to them.

'There, it's all over now,' Mrs Hammond comforted her, and as a great wave of dizziness swept over her,

Tara heard Mrs Hammond's anxious voice appealing to James to catch her.

When she opened her eyes she was lying on a watered silk bedspread in a room decorated in palest eau-de-nil, Mrs Hammond hovering anxiously on one side while James stood, tall and saturnine, on the other.

'The twins . . .'

'They're both fast asleep,' James reassured her. 'You can go and check for yourself if you like. It would be pointless waking them now,' he added, glancing at his watch. 'It's gone ten now . . . You might as well stay the night and then I can run you all home in the morning.'

Tara wanted to protest, but Mrs Hammond was already agreeing, murmuring something about coming in a little earlier in the morning to cope with breakfast.

'Mrs Hammond doesn't sleep in,' James told her, correctly reading her mind. 'But you're quite safe.' Mrs Hammond had obviously not overheard the comment and James's eyes were sardonic as he murmured the words.

On shaky legs, Tara followed him to the room the twins were sharing. The two of them were tucked up in a large double bed. Tara bent to kiss them unable to resist the urge to touch them. Mandy opened her eyes, happiness filling them as she smiled drowsily, her smothered 'Mummy' balm to Tara's aching heart.

James made no attempt to ignore the tears pouring down her face as she left the bedroom, but Tara was beyond caring. Relief coursed through her, drowning out every other emotion, including the dragging tiredness she had experienced during the day.

James left her at the door of the eau-de-nil room. The bedroom had its own adjoining bathroom, tiled in the same soft green, the bath reflecting the colour like a huge mother-of-pearl shell. Perfumed bath oil and soft fluffy towels hinted that she wasn't the first female to use this room, and Tara had to smother a swift stab of jealousy. She was being ridiculous, she told herself. Any woman James had staying in his home would surely share his room and not sleep alone. No wonder Mrs Hammond did not live in. It had been plain to Tara that she thought very highly of her employer, and no doubt James fostered that impression.

She was still wearing the old jeans she had put on that morning—a lifetime ago—and her tee-shirt was stained with oil from changing the car wheel. When she looked at her reflection in the mirror she was appalled at the dishevelled, untidy picture that met her eyes. Her hair curled wildly round her face, unusually pale, her eyes dark pools of pain, her mouth free of lipstick. Distastefully Tara removed her jeans and the grubby tee-shirt. Beneath them she was only wearing a pair of briefs and a flimsy lace bra. Faced with the prospect of donning worn clothes in the morning, she shuddered. At least she could rinse her underclothes through; being nylon they would dry overnight, and she had started on her self-imposed chore before she realised that she had nothing to sleep in.

Shrugging she started to run her bath, helping herself to a generous capful of the expensively perfumed oil, the warm water helped to soothe away some of her tension, but Tara did not linger in the bath. All at once she was swept by exhaustion and knew that if she didn't make an effort to reach the bed she was likely to fall asleep where she was.

Drying herself on one of the luxuriously thick towels, she padded across to the bed and was just pulling back the bedclothes when, with only a brief knock, James came into the room. In one hand he was holding a pair of pyjamas, and Tara felt the blood rising betrayingly under her skin as he looked at her, his eyes lingering longest on the rounded swell of her breasts above the confining edge of her towel.

'I realised you had nothing with you, and I brought you these,' he told her, proffering the pyjamas. Tara reached forward to take them, keeping a tight grip of her towel, feeling herself tremble beneath his gaze.

'What's wrong?' he jeered. 'Surely you're not shy. You've been married and widowed, had lovers . . .'

His words were designed to be insulting and some spark of defiance Tara hadn't known she possessed stirred her into saying coolly, 'What are you trying to do? Ease your conscience because you took my virginity?'

'Took it?' The dark eyebrows rose, his mouth tightening in a thin, cruel line. 'I don't recall that there was much taking involved—or is that the line you perfected for your husband? Work hard at it and you might even be able to convince yourself that it was rape. That's the next step, isn't it? But we both know that wasn't the case, don't we?'

'It wasn't rape, perhaps, but it was deliberate seduction,' Tara countered, too angry to care what she was saying, 'and in my book that's nearly as bad.'

'Time seems to have affected your memory,' James

drawled, only the dark line of colour along his cheekbones warning her that he was fighting to control his temper. 'As I recall it, we were both equal partners.' His eyes dropped again to her breasts, his soft, 'Perhaps I ought to refresh your memory as it's so badly at fault,' freezing the blood in Tara's veins. She moved backwards instinctively, wincing as she felt the hard frame of the bed behind her knees, one hand going up instinctively to ward off the implacable male frame, but James ignored her. Unwilling to bear the contempt in his eyes, she closed her own, tensing as she waited for those hard hands to wrench away her frail protection, but the assault never came. Instead she felt James's hands on her shoulders, stroking and massaging away the tension of the day, encouraging her head to fall forward heavily on to his chest as one arm slid round her back to support her. The rhythmic stroking continued, lulling her into a false sense of security, no protest escaping her lips as James's hands moved gently over her back relaxing taut muscles.

At first the sure touch of his fingers was simply relaxing, but then, gradually, other feelings sprang to life inside her. Beneath the towel Tara felt her breasts swell and tauten, her arms automatically encircling James's neck, her fingers burrowing into the soft thickness of his hair.

She felt him lift her on to the bed but was beyond making any form of protest. She wanted this sense of closeness, this union of flesh against flesh, this sense of desiring and being desired, and she refused to let any other emotion intrude.

Somehow her hands found their way inside the opening of his shirt, clinging to the moist warmth of his skin, exploring the maleness of his body with a sensuality she had never possessed at seventeen. Then she had merely gloried in her love; simply accepting the physical perfection of their coming together, but now, with experience on her side, Tara was well aware of the intense male virility of James's body, of the strength in the broad shoulders and tapering chest, of the sensual pleasure to be had from pressing her palms against the fine dark hair shadowing his chest and feeling its slight rasp against her skin.

Now it was his mouth that stroked erotically against her skin, probing the hollow at the base of her throat, moving upwards to investigate the perfect delicacy of her ear before tracing the shape of her cheekbone while his thumb probed the half parted softness of her mouth, sending waves of pleasure shuddering through her body.

Her fingers tugged at the buttons denying her access to the contact she craved with his skin, a small moan of pleasure stifled in her throat as James possessed her mouth, obliterating everything but the driving need to respond to the male pressure of his body, the tautly muscled potency of his thighs as he moulded her body to his, her impatient fingers at last able to push aside his shirt and explore the vital maleness of his skin.

The fear she had experienced during the day seemed to have released her from normal convention and restraints. Husky moans breathed against the tanned column of his throat as her lips explored its warm contours only incited James to increase his subtle torture of her aching body. Her towel was tugged firmly away, her breath catching in her throat as James bent his head to stroke softly over the aroused pink tips of her breasts, with lips that teased and tormented before giving an exquisite pleasure that tied her stomach muscles in knots and sent a wild desire burning along her veins, her fingernails scoring the smooth flesh of his back as her body responded to his touch.

When it came to lovemaking, James was a master of the art, Tara acknowledged hazily, as he caressed the slender length of her thighs, inciting her to writhe wantonly against him, her fingers trembling as they followed the downward path of dark body hair to the belt fastened snugly above his hips. In James's face, Tara could see the desire she knew must be in her own. As he reached for his belt, he muttered something, a tide of darkly red colour running up under his skin as he demanded hoarsely, 'You do it for me,' his hand guiding hers to the metal buckle.

Twenty-four hours ago she could never have imagined herself in such a situation, and the girl she had once been would have shied away from such a request. But she was not a girl any more, she was a woman, and while James had been her only lover the instinct she had been taught to subdue as a teenager now came to the fore, guiding her now. She heard James's stifled gasp of pleasure and felt the shudder that ran through his body when her fingertips brushed the vulnerable flesh of his stomach, with a tiny thrill of pleasure, bending her head to place light kisses where her fingers had touched, glorying in his unmistakable response, although she wasn't given long to exult in her brief ascendancy.

With a swiftness that left her breathless she was jerked against the pulsating male body, her mouth captured and subjected to the burning pressure of male lips that seemed determined to imprint their texture and desire against hers in a way that she could never forget, the hardened thrust of James's body as he parted her thighs and slid between them driving every sensation but the need for his possession completely from her mind.

The silken brush of flesh against flesh was unbearably arousing. Her stomach clenched instinctively, her body aching for the pleasure it knew instinctively James would give. They kissed and clung, stroking feverishly, feeding the furnace of desire they were both feeling. James's control was the greater. Feeling she could stand it no more, Tara pressed herself wantonly against him, murmuring her need against his mouth, her fingers twining in the silky darkness of his hair. They were wrenched rudely away, and icy shivers coursed through her body as the mantle of passion dropped from James like a borrowed cloak.

Cupping her face between his hands so that she was forced to meet the scorn in his eyes, he glanced slowly along the slender paleness of her body. By the time his gaze returned to her face, it was awash with colour.

'Now,' he said softly, no vestige of passion or desire left, 'now tell me again how it was between us. Tell me the way you told the man you married. Tell me that you never really wanted me.'

# CHAPTER TEN

THANK goodness, even now she was not sure how she had managed to pack it in, Tara reflected, studying the bulging boot to the car. A quick glance over her shoulder assured her that the twins were playing happily in the garden. Since the day they had run away she had to fight against a tendency to be too over-protective with them.

She had been too keyed up and anxious that morning at James's house to talk to them, but afterwards when they were all home she had spoken to them both carefully, warning them of some of the risks they had run and reassuring them that the loss of her teapot meant nothing.

Mrs Hammond had been all sympathy. She had brought Tara breakfast in bed, telling her a brief anecdote about her own daughter. 'And it's always the silliest little things that lead to upsets,' she told Tara, plainly aware of the accident to the teapot.

There had been the ordeal of thanking James for his care of the twins to endure, her eyes never moving from the third button of his shirt, her whole body tensed in shame and self-loathing as she tried to blot out memories of the previous night.

'I suppose it's no good my warning you that the twins will never accept Saunders as their father?' was all James said when he had listened to her stumbling speech.

'Who says they're going to be asked to?' Tara fired back, misery giving way to choking anger. 'The twins have a father,' she reminded him, 'and my relationship with Chas is purely my affair.'

'So you don't intend to marry him?'

'Shocked?' The taunt slipped off her tongue. 'How very hypocritical of you! At least Chas and I are free to enter into a relationship with one another.'

'You've changed, Tara,' came the acid response. 'The Tara I knew would never have settled for anything second-rate—or is it simply that your ability to love completely died with your husband?' he demanded with a harshness that shocked her.

Tara laughed mirthlessly. How close he was to the truth, but not in the way he imagined.

'Well?' he probed bitingly.

'When I lost the twins' father I lost almost everything worth having in life,' Tara told him truthfully. 'Now, can I go?'

'Is it time yet?'

Simon was standing on one leg surveying the car hopefully. Both he and Mandy had been thrilled when Tara told them they were going away on holiday. Too young yet to draw comparisons between the holiday they were having and those enjoyed by their schoolmates, they had talked of nothing else for the last three weeks, and Tara had encouraged them, hoping that in their excitement they could all forget the trauma of the afternoon they had run away. Even now she could not come to terms with the pain of it— they had run away to James! She had explained to them both that Chas was her employer and friend, but nothing more, and there had been a noticeable improvement in Mandy's manner towards him ever since. In fact the only cloud on the little girl's horizon was the absence of her beloved 'Uncle James'. On several occasions she had begged Tara to telephone him, worried because he had not been round to see them, and Tara had explained as gently as she could that James had his own life to live. But now they were off to Dartmoor for a fortnight, and Tara was determined that nothing was going to spoil what amounted to the first proper holiday she and the twins had ever had.

The drive down to the cottage was relatively uneventful. They stopped to eat the packed lunch Tara had prepared, just off the motorway, before resuming their journey, and it was just gone six when at last they turned on to the rutted track leading to the cottage.

It was just as Tara had visualised, one of a pair crouched beneath overhanging eaves, its grey stone walls grizzled with age and smothered in pale cream roses.

A smiling, plump woman in her thirties emerged from the adjoining cottage as Tara followed the twins out of the car.

'Hi,' she greeted them, 'I'm Margaret Burton, your new temporary neighbour. Fancy a cup of tea, or would you prefer to be left alone to settle in?'

Seeing that the twins were already eyeing the large and friendly-looking mongrel dog that had followed Margaret out of her cottage with interest, Tara accepted.

Over tea she learned that the Burtons had been

coming to Dartmoor for several years.

'Of course now that the kids are growing up they're beginning to show an interest in more exotic venues—we took them to Paris at Easter and we're spending a week in Holland later in the year; they're just reaching that stage where they're beginning to tire of the beach, so we're force-feeding them with a little culture.' She chuckled as she spoke and glanced at the twins before saying warmly, 'Your two will love it here, I'm sure. It isn't far to the coast, and there are some wonderful beaches. My husband will be back with our three shortly. They've gone into Dartmouth on a shopping spree—we're here for a month this time and needed to re-provision. Once you've settled in we must go out for a drink together one evening. Gill, my eldest, is fourteen and well trained as a baby-sitter, if you fancy the idea.'

By the time Tara got up to leave she felt as though she had made a friend, as had the twins with the Burtons' family pet, Robot, as the large mongrel was somewhat improbably named.

By the time she had prepared a light meal, discovered how the Calor gas cooker and other equipment worked, and unpacked the car, it was almost time for bed. A quick shower in the minute but attractive bathroom still damp from the twins' baths, and her eyes closed the moment her head touched the pillow.

It must be something to do with the country air, Tara decided drowsily the following morning when she opened her eyes to sunshine and bird song. She couldn't remember when she had last enjoyed such a deep and untroubled sleep. The morning was warm and languorous, and she experienced a feeling of letting go, of relaxing in a way she had not done in years; not since the twins' birth, she admitted to herself, a little disconcerted to realise how tense she had actually become without knowing it, unaware of each further winding of her already over-stretched nerves until her tension was something she had learned to live with.

The first two days of their holiday were spent exploring their environs. There were plenty of attractive walks close at hand, the twins' favourite being to the farm, where they went every morning with the Burton children to collect milk and eggs. The farmer who owned the cottages called to check that they had everything they wanted, and warned Tara in a very friendly way about the danger of allowing the children to run free on the moor—something she had no intention of doing, and when he discovered how fascinated Simon was by the farm and its animals he invited them all to spend a morning there.

Simon returned starry-eyed and ecstatic. He had actually been allowed to touch a week-old calf, all wobbly-legged and big-eyed; Mandy had preferred the ponies, sturdy moorland creatures which ran free on the moorland pastures.

On the third day of their holiday Tara packed the twins and their swimming gear into the car and on the Burtons' suggestion drove to a beach they had recommended as being ideally suited for children.

They saw the sea long before they reached it, unbelievably blue, tiny waves shimmering silver under the clear sky.

The tiny bay—it was really nothing more—was

reached by descending steep steps cut into the cliffside, but once reached it more than repaid the effort involved. The cliffs sheltered the bay from the light breeze, heat bouncing off the pale golden sand. Only a dozen or so other families had braved the steps, and Tara was glad to see that the beach was completely free of icecream sellers and the like and completely uncommercialised.

Both the twins could swim, but Tara made sure that they never entered the water without her. Watching them playing together like baby seals, their newly tanned bodies gleaming with the seawater, she experienced an overwhelming need to share the moment with James; to exchange with him a look of doting parenthood over their oblivious heads. Pain swept her, her eyes drawn involuntarily to the other families on the beach; complete units, mothers and fathers with their children. She was being foolish, she warned herself; she was an adult and knew better than to fall into the trap of the 'perfection' of family life, and yet the pain inside her wouldn't go away. She closed her eyes on betraying tears, shocked by the images shimmering against her eyelids of herself and James, lying together beneath the hot sun, his hands on her body. Forcing the images away, she tried to concentrate on the present, to blot out all memories of the past, on her love for James, and her yearning need to have him with her.

Margaret had been marvellous about not asking questions, and although Tara had been a little perturbed when she first discovered the cottage was not on its own, she admitted now that she was glad of a little adult company, especially when it was as unobtrusive as Margaret and Sam's.

The twins too, had made fast friends with the Burtons' two younger children, Philip and Robert, aged ten and twelve respectively, while Gill made no secret of the fact that she adored the twins.

'You wait,' Margaret had predicted gloomily, watching her with them. 'This year it's kids, next it will be boys!'

Later in the afternoon Tara drove into Dartmouth to do some shopping. She bought postcards to send to Chas and Janice, and was amused when Mandy announced importantly that she too had postcards to write and asked for stamps to stick on them.

Her school friends, no doubt, Tara decided, passing over the requisite stamps. Poor little girl, this was the first opportunity she had had to send rather than receive, and she was obviously determined to make the most of it, even though the stamps were not the exotic variety she received from her friends.

That evening they had supper with the Burtons, and when Margaret suggested that they stroll down to the village pub for a drink, Tara felt relaxed enough to agree.

There was a moment, when she urged the twins to behave themselves for Gill, when she remembered coming home to the shattered teapot and the appalling silence that accompanied it, but she banished it firmly, reminding herself how she had always striven to allow the twins some measure of independence. Simon had disconcerted her by clinging a little to Sam Burton, and watching him blossom and gain confidence as he copied the Burton boys she had experienced a twinge of fear that she was depriving him of the male influence he seemed to need.

It was a pleasant walk to the pub—crowded with holidaymakers and locals, and Tara thoroughly enjoyed the hour or so they spent there before walking back, although she couldn't help noticing on the return journey how Margaret slipped her hand companionably into Sam's, and the teasing smile they exchanged. A great sense of desolation overwhelmed her. She had to stop feeling like this, she warned herself. She simply could not succumb to morbid envy every time she witnessed intimacy between another couple.

The days passed pleasantly, the good weather holding. They toured the moors one day and ate a picnic lunch in the shade of a tumbledown cottage, Simon entranced by the sturdy ponies who watched them inquisitive and greedy. All three of them were tanned, scarcely recognisable from the city dwellers who had arrived such a short time ago. They must try and do this every year, Tara decided as she set the car in motion. It had done them all good.

The following day Margaret announced that they were visiting a nearby safari park and invited the twins to go with them.

'I won't suggest that you come,' she told Tara. 'Have a day on your own. Read a book, laze about. Something tells me you don't get many opportunities to be alone.'

Silently blessing Margaret for her kindness, Tara passed on the invitation to the twins. As she had suspected, they were thrilled, and although she felt a tiny pang when she saw how blithely unconcerned they were that she was not to accompany them, she told herself that it was only right and natural. Simon in particular had been too clinging.

They left after breakfast, waving enthusiastically to her from the Burtons' Range Rover.

When they had gone Tara washed up and made the beds before unearthing a book she had brought with her. If anything the weather had improved, today the sun shone from a cloudless sky with only the merest suggestion of a breeze. Donning her bikini, Tara wandered into the attractive cottage-style garden at the back of the cottage. After a while her book failed to hold her attention. She could hear a bee humming drowsily nearby, and a pleasant lethargy crept over her. She closed her eyes.

Footsteps crunching on the gravel woke her. She sat up, swivelling round to see the intruder, then all the breath left her lungs on a painful gasp as her eyes travelled incredulously upwards over lean, jean-clad thighs to James's dark inscrutable face.

For a moment she thought she must be hallucinating and that her dreams had conjured him up out of nowhere. She blinked, dazzled by the sunlight bouncing off his sunglasses, wishing he would remove them so that she could at least see his eyes. He moved, and the thin body-hugging shirt exposed the fluid muscles of his torso.

'James!' Her voice ached over his name. 'What . . . what are you doing here?—How did you know where to find us?'

'Mandy sent me a postcard.' The grimness round his mouth seemed to relax a little. 'She put your address on it, but I would have found you anyway, if it had meant searching every inch of the country.' He removed his glasses and Tara shrank from the anger she saw blazing in his eyes.

'How could you?' he breathed, walking towards her, his stance almost menacing as he towered over her. She longed to scramble to her feet, but something kept her where she was, her heart pounding in longing and fear.

With a swiftness that startled her he dropped down beside her, so close that she could see the faint shadow along his jaw where he had shaved. A need to reach out and touch him overwhelmed her, but she refused to succumb to it.

'Did you honestly hate me that much?' he demanded, his voice curiously uneven. 'So much that you kept the existence of my own children from me?'

Tara was too stunned to speak, but any hopes she had nourished of denying his allegation were quenched as he grasped her shoulders, almost shaking her in his anger, his harsh, 'And for God's sake don't compound your crime by denying it; the truth is written all over you, even if I hadn't seen the birth certificates with my own eyes!'

With a crawling sickness Tara's mind swept back to those first despairing days after the twins' birth. She had been too drained and weary to rationalise, too hurt by James's betrayal, and when they had brought her the forms to fill in in the space designated 'father' she had written James's name almost before she realised it.

James's bitter 'Why, damn you?' and the shake that accompanied it dragged her from the past, and her own bitterness welled up to meet his.

'What was I supposed to do?' she cried. 'I was seventeen—what choice did I have? An abortion? I couldn't, and that I was only an amusing interlude to you was made more than clear to me, as I'm sure you'll remember.'

She turned her face away, hating herself for the tell-tale tears rolling down her face, gasping when James grasped her chin, forcing her eyes to meet him.

'Will I?' he asked smoothly. 'You'll have to make allowances for my advancing years, I'm afraid and remind me afresh, starting from the moment you discovered you were pregnant.'

For a moment she was tempted to refuse, hating his cynical attitude. Of course he didn't remember—why should he? To him she was merely one more fool among many. Anger stirred, whipping soft colour into her cheeks.

In a voice that trembled she reminded him of how he had disappeared after they had made love without a word to her, and how she had foolishly believed that he loved her. How terrified she had been when she discovered she was pregnant, how she had plucked up her courage to visit the house, hoping to ask his advice and how she had been met with scorn and mockery when Hilary told her the truth.

'And you told her you were pregnant?'

Tara shook her head proudly. 'There was no point. I knew then that you wouldn't help me, that you'd never meant any of the things ... that you didn't care about me the way I cared about you,' she managed to enunciate clearly.

When she lifted her eyes he was looking away from her, his face set and hard as though it had been carved in granite. He turned his head and the pain and desolation in his eyes took her breath, leaving a tight agony in her chest when she tried to breathe.

'I had no idea,' he said simply. 'And it wasn't like that at all, Tara. God, if you hadn't been so young, so innocent . . . but I didn't want to burden you, to spoil what there was between us. I went away simply to give you a breathing space—to allow you to grow up and discover if what you professed to feel for me was real or imaginary. Can you imagine how I felt? I'd taken your sweet innocence when I had no right. My marriage might have been a farcical sham, but I was still married—although I'd asked Hilary for a divorce long before you and I met. However, my marriage is something we can discuss later. I loved you,' he told her simply. 'Perhaps I had no right, but I did. When you offered me yourself so sweetly I couldn't stop myself although I suffered a hell of bitter regret later. I went away vowing to give you the opportunity to make up your own mind, telling myself that it was only right that you should meet and fall in love with boys your own age, but when I came back and discovered you'd married, I was forced to admit to myself how much I'd been counting on your love, how much I wanted your sweetness, your body against mine.'

Tara swallowed, unable to believe her ears.

'You mean what Hilary told me wasn't true?' she managed to croak at last. 'I wasn't merely one of a long string of brief affairs?'

James shook his head. 'You were the only one—and you weren't a brief affair,' he told her roughly. 'Let me tell you about my marriage. My father owned a small engineering company which he had built up over many years. My mother adored him and when he died

I thought I would lose her too. Up until then I'd never met Hilary, although I knew she owned some shares in the company. She arrived several weeks after my father's death—she spent the weekend with us. I found her glossy and hard. She was the antithesis of everything I looked for in a woman, but she made it plain that she was attracted to me. I was twenty-four and made the mistake of laughing at her.

'She left, and then a week later I received in the post some photo-copies of letters my father had written to her and which made it plain that they were lovers. If I didn't agree to what she wanted she was going to show them to my mother. I was caught in a trap. I knew it would totally destroy my mother to learn the truth—I couldn't really believe that my father had actually loved Hilary, but he had obviously desired her and made love to her, and my gentle mother would never be able to understand.

'I got in touch with Hilary, suspecting that what she had in mind was that I should fill my father's shoes, so to speak. We were having problems with the company at the time. My father had generously given a long-standing employee a block of shares, which meant that he no longer had overall control, and I was desperately trying to buy the shares back. What Hilary had to suggest appalled and infuriated me. An affair wouldn't restore the damage I had caused to her pride, apparently. I had laughed at her and for that she demanded marriage. Oh, I refused—at first, but she's a shrewd and determined woman. She held on to the threat of those letters, and she had almost managed to buy a controlling interest in the company. In the end I capitulated. We were never lovers,' he told Tara bluntly, 'but the mere fact that I'd married her salved her wounded ego. My mother died twelve months after we were married. That was the summer before I met you. I asked Hilary for a divorce and went on asking her, but she refused. It didn't really matter, I knew sooner or later she would take a lover and grow bored with tormenting me, and there was no one else I wanted in my life, until I met you. I tried to hold back, not to sully you with the total mess my life had become, but you were like cool, pure spring water after a surfeit of sour wine, and the more time I spent with you the more I longed for you. I left England determined to give you a chance to grow up unfettered by my desire, and also to insist again that Hilary gave me a divorce. I'd already asked her when she met you.'

Tara had been silent while he spoke, but now tears choked her of breath and she longed to reach out and convey her anguish for him.

'I thought I was going to go mad when I discovered you were married,' James said quietly, 'and for a while perhaps I did. I concentrated on freeing myself from Hilary—I blamed losing you on her. I also managed to buy enough shares to gain control of the business. As I had suspected, Hilary had taken a lover and our divorce eventually went through, and I was a free man again—only I wasn't free, Tara,' he said huskily. 'You haunted me. When Sue told me that she'd met you again I told myself I wasn't going to get involved, that the past was dead and that the sensible thing was to avoid you. She told me that you were a widow with two children. I told myself I didn't want to know, but somehow I found myself urging her to allow me to drive you down to her home. I wanted to feel indifference towards you. I wanted to dislike the twins. I couldn't bear the thought of you giving birth to another man's child, but somehow they destroyed my defences and the hatred I'd expected to feel towards them became channelled towards your dead husband. I was jealous of Chas Saunders, but he was a known rival, something I could contend with, especially when I realised the twins didn't like him. But their father ... And when you kept insisting that you still loved him ...' He broke off suddenly, an arrested expression crossing his face. 'Him, or me, Tara?' he demanded huskily. 'Did you love the man you married to protect the twins, or when you told me you loved their father, did you mean me?'

'For God's sake,' he muttered savagely when she refused to speak, 'stop torturing me like this. Have you any idea what I've been through? Forced into dragging what titbits of information I could out of the twins, trying desperately to build up a mental picture of the man who'd supplanted me, and all the time you resisting me. That's why I went to Somerset House. I thought if I had a name I might be able to discover something about him, instead of which I discovered that I was a father ... Tell me about him, Tara,' he urged. 'What was he like? What ...'

Tara moistened her lips with her tongue, fear a coiled knot inside her. She was about to release her last defence, to expose herself to possible ridicule and pain and yet something drove her on, pushing aside caution.

'He didn't exist,' she answered nervously. 'There was no man, no husband.' She glanced down at the cheap gold wedding ring she wore. 'I made it all up ...

At first I wasn't going to, but men . . . people . . .'

'Were crass enough to believe because you'd been to bed with one man without the benefit of clergy you were willing to do so with more?' James suggested softly. 'Oh, my poor love!' His hands were framing her face, the long fingers trembling slightly against her skin. Like tiny shoots from a vulnerable plant, emotions started to grow inside her, hope flowering in her eyes as she looked up at him.

'About the twins,' he continued. 'Now that I've discovered that I am their father.' He paused expectantly and the light died out of her eyes. Of course he didn't still care about her—she had been a fool to think he might.

'I'm not giving them up,' she said stiffly, tensing her body in preparation for the confrontation to come.

'I'm not asking you to. We can share them.'

'On alternate weekends?' she demanded bitterly.

'I had something a little better than that in mind.'

'Such as?'

'Such as marriage,' James told her softly.

For a moment Tara was silent, and then the pain began.

'You're prepared to go to those lengths to get two children you didn't even know you'd fathered until a matter of days ago?' She injected as much scorn as she could into the words, but James ignored it.

'Them,' he agreed, 'and their mother. Tara, have you any idea what I endured when I returned from the States and discovered you'd gone?' he demanded urgently. 'Oh, I told myself it was all for the best, that I was too old for you, but none of it helped. I tortured myself night after night, imagining you confessing our lovemaking to your husband, dismissing it as just one of those things, when for me the memory of how it had felt to hold you in my arms and taste your first sweet cries of desire was something I could never forget. I loved you then and I love you now,' he said slowly.

'You love me?' Still she couldn't believe it, although hope trembled and grew again, her own love reflected in her eyes as she lifted them to his face. And then as though suddenly words could no longer convey how he felt, James reached for her murmuring against her mouth, 'Perhaps this will convince you,' as he possessed it with all the raw hunger she had dreamed of and which he had kept concealed from her on the other occasions when he had kissed her.

They were completely alone in the garden and she had neither the desire nor the will to resist when he lowered her on to the grass, removing the brief scraps of her bikini, the sun stroking moltenly over her body, before he covered it with his.

Their lovemaking was a white-hot need consuming them both, her body electrically responsive to his touch, his possession a shattering climax to their need for one another.

Later, as long shadows crept across the garden and their voices were drowsy with content, James reached for her again. This time there was tenderness and sensitivity in the drift of his hands over her body; as though both knew and acknowledged that there would be many many times like this when they could give and take pleasure from one another. Tara, revelling in her freedom to touch and draw from him a response he no longer made any attempt to hide, marvelled that she had not seen before that it was more than simply a desire to humiliate her that had driven him to touch her, but she had been held fast in her own despair.

'The twins,' she murmured drowsily, as his fingers cupped her breast, stroking the pale flesh. 'What are we going to tell them?'

James bent his head to place sensuously warm lips against the swelling flesh before answering.

'The truth—when they're old enough to understand,' he said firmly, 'For now let it simply be enough for them that we're going to be married. It's my opinion that fatherhood is something that has to be earned. They like me, and I think will accept me in their lives. It's the man who shows his love by being there during their childhood who merits the term father, not the one who gives them life!'

Tara knew he was right. Mandy would be ecstatic to have James as her father, and so would Simon in his quieter way, and as James had said, there was time enough to tell them the truth when they were old enough to accept it. She looked down at the dark head pillowed against her breast, and love stirred inside her, her fingertips moved sensitively over a bronzed shoulder, pleasure curling through her as she felt James's warm breath against her skin.

'Love me?'

James raised his head and smiled teasingly, 'Is that a question or an invitation? Either way the answer is yes. Do you love me?'

Happiness flowed through her veins like wine, making her lightheaded. 'More than words can say,' she told him. 'Shall I show you?'

His answer was in the kiss they shared, the rising

need she felt in his body, the urgency of his hands as they caressed her willing flesh. She remembered how she had fantasised about making love with him on the beach such a short time ago, believing the reality impossible. She grinned inwardly. Not tomorrow but perhaps tomorrow night she might suggest a walk along that moon-drenched sand.

'Why are you smiling?' James demanded against her lips.

'Because I'm so happy,' she told him simply, and responded joyously to his murmured, 'Show me.'

## A SHAKESPEAREAN SONNET

Like many of us, Tara, Penny Jordan's heroine, is able to find escape from worries and pressures in the pages of a book. Tara's particular joy is "the heady pleasure of Shakespeare's sonnets." We've reprinted below "My Mistress' Eyes Are Nothing like the Sun," a sonnet we think is one of the more interesting and enjoyable ones penned by William Shakespeare, renowned English dramatist and poet of 400 years ago.

My mistress' eyes are nothing like the sun;
Coral is far more red than her lips' red;
If snow be white, why then her breasts are dun;
If hairs be wires, black wires grow on her head.
I have seen roses damasked red and white,
But no such roses see I in her cheeks;
And in some perfumes is there more delight
Than in the breath that from my mistress reeks.
I love to hear her speak, yet well I know
That music hath a far more pleasing sound;
I grant I never saw a goddess go;
My mistress, when she walks, treads on the ground.
And yet, by heaven, I think my love as rare
As any she belied with false compare.

# What the press says about Harlequin romance fiction...

"When it comes to romantic novels...
Harlequin is the indisputable king."
—*New York Times*

" 'Harlequin [is]... the best and the biggest.' "
—*Associated Press* (quoting Janet Dailey's husband, Bill)

"The most popular reading matter of
American women today."
—*Detroit News*

"... exciting escapism, easy reading, interesting
characters and, always, a happy ending....
They are hard to put down."
—*Transcript-Telegram*, Holyoke (Mass.)

"... a work of art."
—*Globe & Mail*, Toronto